FOR SUCH A LONG TIME, SHE HAD
KEPT HER GIFT
A SECRET—
BUT IF SHE HELPED THIS MAN . . .

"I dreamed you could do it," he said. "God touches those that's got the power, Mum. Ah kin see it in yo eyes, don't you know. Ah kin see it."

Florice closed her eyes and sighed. Her senses told her he had syphilis and her common sense told her that she should send him away, but something held her there. She remembered the light in her hands.

"These sores, Mam. If you could just pray over em a leetle bit? I don repented, and I's been born again, an I still ain't well atall."

She moved toward him and put her coffee on the table. "Before I do this, you must promise me not to tell anyone. . . ."

Also by Linda Beatrice Brown:

A LOVE SONG TO BLACK MEN

RAINBOW ROUN MAH SHOULDER

Linda Beatrice Brown

BALLANTINE BOOKS · NEW YORK

to Yvonne and Elizabeth,
the Keepers of the rainbow

The publication of *Rainbow Roun Mah Shoulder* is made possible, in
part, by grants from the North Carolina Arts Council and the National
Endowment for the Arts, a federal agency.

Library of Congress Catalog Card Number: 84-17045

ISBN 0-345-35876-7

This edition published by arrangement with Carolina Wren Press

Manufactured in the United States of America

First Ballantine Books Edition: February 1989

Though I speak with the tongues of men and of angels, and have not charity, I am become as a sounding brass, or a tinkling cymbal. And though I have the gift of prophecy and understand all mysteries, and all knowledge; and though I have all faith so that I could remove mountains, and have not charity, I am nothing. And though I bestow all my goods to the poor, and though I give my body to the burned, and have not charity, it profiteth me nothing. Charity suffereth long, and is kind; charity envieth not; charity vaunteth not itself, is not puffed up, doth not behave itself unseemly, seeketh not her own, is not easily provoked, thinketh no evil; rejoiceth not in iniquity, but rejoiceth in the truth; beareth all things, believeth all things, hopeth all things, endureth all things. Charity never faileth: but whether there be prophecies, they shall fail; whether there be tongues, they shall cease; whether there be knowledge it shall vanish away. For we know in part and we prophesy in part. But when that which is perfect is come, then that which is in part shall be done away. When I was a child, I spake as a child, I understood as a child, I thought as a child: but when I became a man, I put away childish things. For now we see through a glass darkly; but then face to face: now I know in part; but then shall I know even as also I am known. And now abideth faith, hope, charity, these three; but the greatest of these is charity.

CORINTHIANS 1:13

1915

Cup of tea; it was New Orleans hot but she was cold. Her hair felt cold when she brushed it off her forehead. Cup of tea. If it were winter, she'd have a fire. Mac was probably on his way home. She wanted to convince him that a move to North Carolina would be good for them. She wanted a family. Her sister was there, and maybe she'd get in the family way and make him happy. She went into the bedroom and got her shawl. She had to go somewhere far away from Theodore. She had been frightened for him and of him for the last couple of weeks—his dark eyes looked dead and his hands looked gray. Where was he? Where was he, with his faith? They had sat in the church office while he talked nervously of his faith almost as if it were an animal that had been domesticated and could go wild. "Votive candles are for a kind of wishing," he had said. Speech from him combined the magic of incantation with the knowledge that he had a certain power over people.

"And what you wish for to the angels?" she had said. There was a long silence.

"Whatever you feel is both thorn and berry, as that is the nature of life." That was it, why he had always fascinated her, mystified her. "As that is the nature of life." He did have a way of talking. They had walked through all the Catholic churches in town while he explained the different objects—church furniture, he had said, and she had thought that was a peculiar name to call pews and such.

Theodore, Father Theodore Canty. His arms had been warm and not at all seductive but it felt like home when his welcome back embrace covered her empty spaces. Where do

I go from here? she thought. My Lord, what do I do now? He wasn't all Black, not Black actin' or Black lookin'. His mama was some kinda Black Indian and his dead daddy had kept Theodore a secret from all the good parishioners at St. Ignatius.

She saw him as often as she could possibly see him. There was some visceral excitement she had never had with Mac or any of the boys in the parish before marriage. It was not that seeing him was dangerous, which it was, it was not that she hoped for anything with him really, but there was with him an understanding of her nature, her passion, her yearning toward the mystical, her quiet, rumbling store, that kept pushing her not so gently toward that great river he called God.

He was frightened; she was controlled raging, and it would soon be over. She would lose what she had never had. She remembered it a long time later, as the first time. A numbness in the stomach and deeper and deeper, whenever things to come crept up on her mind. Later she would start and then pray when she felt that feeling, but then it was too early for her to recognize that knowing when something was going to live also meant that you had to know when something was going to die. Rebecca closed her eyes.

There was a heat that she felt more and more now, with Mac refusing to sleep with her. Thorn and berry-red flashed before her eyes. There was a beautiful pain in her desire. Father Canty had lit the candle in one whose feelings were strong enough to lead her to attempt murder and to consider the veil. Some day, she would understand that she could be both murderer and nun, and she would accept the gift. The thorn was sweet, it twisted in her mouth like a sharp gold wire that ran from the place where the breastbone began at the neck, to the opening of her womb. It is all right, it is all right to feel the thorn move it is all right it is all right it is the pain and the ache of the green blade pushing at the sun it is the heaviness of the tongue where it is thirsty, it is the sweet milk, the moan the body cries that she suppressed when she saw Theodore lift the host and his delicate wrists showed at the edge of his surplice. It is this same gold wire that runs down her thighs and turns to water at the knees. It twisted in her mouth, it sharpened. The thorn and berry moved, trembled in the wind, thorns turned to running red and running and running sun running sun it is all right it is all right it is all it is all golden wine wire on berry bone thorn and berry what you wish, what you wish for to the angels she said what you wish for . . . to . . . the . . . angels . . .

She slept, wrapped in her heat, shocked, frightened, and with joy that reached above the clouds.

The French clock her great-grandmother inherited from the slavers kept time. It was six o'clock. Still heavy, still moist air. Rebecca knocked into the table's edge and bruised her hip. She swore silently in French. Her skin was the color of English walnuts and she had that Creole look that most Black men went wild over. Her full lips were definitely Black and her nose French. She was called a "handsome" woman, too tall to be a cute little thing. Rebecca fingered the lace doily her mother had given her for a wedding present. Hand-crocheted, sitting under a pitcher of sweet William from the backyard. For a few minutes she was lost in the texture of the doily. The tea began to sing and at the same time she heard Mac's step.

"Evenin'." That was it. Formal. Because you're here I'll speak.

"Dinner's on the stove, Mac." She spoke to his chest as if she couldn't get past his neck with her eyes.

"Ain't hungry, girl."

"You ain't never hungry no more." She wrapped her blue shawl tight about her shoulders.

"An' you ain't never warmin' nothin' up."

He would never understand. Not ever. But he had always loved her tallness, her long legs and her tall spirit.

"Mac, let's go away from here."

"Go away, what you mean, Rebecca? Where we gon go? And with what?"

"Mac, my sister's got a place up in North Carolina, and she say it good jobs up there in the mills, and God knows you ain't got no reason to stay here in these cane fields. Ain't nothin' down here but rich white folks, poor niggers and heat. Please, Mac, please."

Something in the pleading, in the voice that spoke of pain and growing and desperate searching, made him wonder if going away would give him back his wife. This old furniture and this three-room house was all he had. New place, new job, maybe she'd love him again.

Rebecca saw his hands unclench. He patted her shoulder. "All right, Miss Letenielle," (he always called her that when she'd won a round) "can't lose without tryin'." For the first time that night, she met his eyes. The clock struck seven o'clock. Time to go play for the church choir practice. Her shawl had fallen off her shoulders. As she bent to pick it up, Mac noticed the fullness of her breasts as they fell forward. He reached to touch for the first time in many days and knocked over the sweet William.

"I'll be back before nine," she shouted as the flimsy screen slammed. The water trickled off the starched doily and onto the floor.

The choir sounded thin, thin like winter sunshine, thin like a poor excuse for a lie. She was glad when it was eight o'clock and they broke up for the night. Father Canty had said the Agnus Dei should be sweet but not so plaintive, God didn't want humble pie. She folded the music slowly and put it under the organ seat. Any minute now he'd come in with his black soutane. "Like a dress," Mac always said, didn't seem right to him, never. She always hated to hear him say that. It gave her the creeps because she knew how much there was of Theodore that was both woman and man.

She heard his step as he turned off lights in the vestry and came out to the sanctuary, in a hurry, anxious.

"So you're still here." He was horrified. What he had planned to do that night, he really had to do because she was still there. His voice was shaped of granite. It carried minute edges of fear, love and pain. She waited quietly on the organ bench. Only the hem of her long skirt shook and the mouth lines, that were later to be vestiges of suffering, showed, as if in prophecy. She sat very still.

He spoke, and the votive candles flickered with his wind

breath. "My love, has it come to this?" Bent over, as if lighting a flame, really to keep from looking at her face, golden, in the dimness of the church. "It is not the sex I want, it is the heat that comes through the trembling hands, the heart that drains away and leaves an open sore. It is you who belong to God, not me. You are the real priest. I would be demoned forever, doomed to stare into an open grave, your face at the bottom, for an eternity."

Sinews, arteries, bones were being loosed from each other. She sat still, he could not see the awful movement of her blood or hear the cavernous echo in her ear—"It is you who belong to God, you who belong." You know the truth when it is spoken to you from the mouth of another—your own thoughts like an echo. She had already said it to herself for as long as that part of her brain allowed her to remember, only now she heard it with her whole brain, and for the first time it was real. The words carried blood and firelight. Her "no" was stopped on the way out of her mouth by some power in her throat and his hand on her mouth. "No, Rebecca. I do not wish to stare into your grave forever, I do not wish it."

Suffering comes in many disguises, but often in such a way that we are caught as if by a thunderstorm whose warnings we have shut away deliberately, as if by shutting the windows to our own little cottages, we have bolted down the house and the storm will not come. So this was suffering. She thought it would be excruciating pain, blood, guts, violent disease, anything but a numbness that felt like the clove oil her granny had put on rotten teeth that had to be pulled. This humming hurt that swelled up from below and slowly boiled to the surface. He dropped his hand, and backed down the altar steps. She had not even acknowledged his presence. She had a sudden impulse to ask him why they used so much marble in Catholic churches. Rebecca heard him close the vestry door, heard the key in the lock, and the silence finally shook her into movement. She rose quickly, scraping the organ bench backwards, went toward the candles, and blew them all out, every wish, every wish; a dream gone bad, she thought, is worse than no dream at all. The scratching in her stomach did not lie. That was all, she thought, all she could count on now.

There are four distinct stages in the metamorphosis of the butterfly. The egg hatches into larva which feeds, grows and molts several times before transforming into a pupa.

* * *

They were to go north by train in the Jim Crow section. There hadn't been too much to pack. Mac's one suit he would wear, and there was a carpetbag apiece, and a few boxes of things handed down from the French ones. Marie had said she'd be there in Jacksonville when they pulled in. Mac had been touchy but sweet; Rebecca Florice complained of woman's miseries all week and seemed to him to move around sleepy-like. She was not there, not for him, and his instinct told him that the mulatto priest was at the heart of it. What was it that made her eyes dull and her young back sag? Was she in a family way? She would only shake her head and think, How could I be? You have to feel somethin' more'n I'm feeling to get a baby.'' That was it, if he only knew. She wasn't feelin' nothin', not the glory, not the windful excitement of shakin' trees between her legs, not the white Light of God's love—nothin'. What was she doin' this for? There was no way for a woman to do what *she* was born to do; there was no way to climb to the top of the fiery furnace and try out your heart. It was a woman's place to have woman's pain always.

On the night before they were to leave New Orleans, be-fore they were to leave this place where they had been mar-ried forever, she built a fire with all the wood they had left. She couldn't seem to get warm anymore. From the day she had said, or rather hadn't said, goodbye to Theodore, she hadn't been able to get warm. The fire was one of many she had built that hot March. Rain had come, too, like the springs of heaven over-flowin', she thought, but she was glad. It suited her. Rain. On the heart's beating drum, on the hurt that ran down the street's gutter. Rain on, cause I don't wanna see no sun 'less my light's on inside.

With that last bit of wood she tried to warm herself. Her last night in the town that yearly celebrated the mystery of sacrifice with total abandon. Rebecca had left her lavender dress out till Thursday because it had a stain on it and she thought she might as well wear it to pack in. As she coughed in some of the smoke from her starting fire, the rising flame flickered on the still more purple stain. A wine stain that had never come out. Back in the vestry at St. Ignatius, she had dropped a decanter and spilled the communion wine. Something she had never brought herself to tell him. The stain reminded her that that omission had never been corrected. As she stared at the stain it seemed to become more important than it really was. It was permanent, she thought, shifting her eyes away, uncomfortable at the thought that there would always be the outline on the floor, running down the sides of her sleeve, down her hem, soaked into the wood people would walk on for a hundred more years, ground into the dirt beneath the feet of whatever priests would come in later years to serve the communion wine at St. Ignatius. The waste was outlined as surely as if she had said, Here is a permanent reminder of what we will never be. She trembled with the paper she had used to start her fire. Dear God, where are you now for me? How do I manage to see unless through Theodore, and where oh where do I go from here? No tears, please don't let me do that. Rain on. Cause I don't wanna see no sun 'less my light's on inside. Rain. But the fire rose up in hot transparency, and somewhere behind her breastbone a shape, like the stain on the dress was purple on purple was red on orange and the sun began to shine on the inside, against her will. No, it can't be. Lordy, Lordy, no . . . and she rocked in a rhythm of disbelief and overwhelming love for the fear itself she felt. No. What he had said was, ''It is you, you who are the real priest,'' and she had thought he was just a coward. The sun behind her breasts grew hot and the words were given. Blessed with power. You. Blessed with power. Heal. Heal and love. You are blessed with power. Heat blew out of the fire. She stretched out her hands and took it as the voice in her head commanded.

Rain on the vine. Spill the rain and be at peace. Rain on

the vine. Who was to be for others a fountain, let the waters flow. She touched her face for the healing of those tears and to remember the gift of rain. Rainbow light glimmered in her head. Her breath came quickly and she rose from before the fire, suddenly needing to move. To see if it had cleared. She opened the front door, wanting really to reach out, wanting the rush of wind. Rain's leftovers trickled off the moss-hung trees and the moon was still covered but glowed behind a large mass of whitish clouds. She stood in the doorway for a good five minutes breathing in the peace, shut the door quietly and crossed the narrow empty room. Unaware of the gift of the rainbow that hung on her, a sign that the light inside was burning like a private sun, the light just beginning to be understood by her, always a mystery, and to be seen in this life by only one other person.

Of course, her fear whispered, she was dumbfounded at losing Theodore. It had not really been a voice from God knows where telling her to heal. How could she do anything like that? People would think she was crazy for sure. She had always been kind of strange, feeling outside the world of wives and children—not getting pregnant when all the other ones did. But this was scary, even to her. After it was over, when she woke up after the rain and remembered, she remembered first the stone that sank in the lake of her insides, and then the strange fire and moonlight; she shook a little in fear of what there was to face out there—the grief and the mission, and dismissing one because it was the only way she could rise from the bed that day. She had pushed the less known emotion to the side of her mind, and until now, the train ride had forced her to peer to the right and left of her thinking. Her mind darted around the gift like a firefly. Afraid to accept, afraid to reject, and finally resting on anger. So. What was she to be? How was she to do anything for God with this plodding man, and this woman's pain? She didn't really ask for this. She hadn't really ever asked for anything, she had only expected love. Afraid of hope, she kept to her inward shadows, averting her eyes from the promise.

''Damn nonsense'' she said under her breath. The wheels clacked and dimmed, clacked and dimmed. Mac snored.

Love makes you think strange and awful things, she thought. A bug crawled up the side of her mind. If I were home, they'd say I'd been fixed by somebody's hoodoo. She jerked her head slightly, wanting to run from the memory of that, but before she knew it she was standing again on the edge of the circle at the ceremonial in New Orleans, the dancers, the fire and the fearful butterfly vision were with her again. The shadows closed, practicing a predestined dance. They made themselves into shapes she had seen at other times, frightening shapes of nightmare hours that now seemed seductive. She got lost in the shadows swaying to the drums, hands, feet; sucking in her core. They were shadows of her mother, long dead; her father's voice called in a distant note of some old agony; she shivered. This had nothing to do with her, this scene of fire and seduction. These weren't her people after all. They were not. They were not . . . but she did belong and why did she? She'd lost her footing and was following a shadow that fluttered around her head. There was musty incense everywhere, and black candles floating in pools of purplish water. Her hands were cold and dry. Pools and pools of water. Something was going through her skull. She felt herself being called; sucked up through her own heart, and the shadow flapped over her, a gorgeous bat, like the princely scarab beetle. The wings turned and the shadow moved into a butterfly shape and rose and rose from her head. She saw her own body form on the wall opposite her; the drums took her last conscious will and the strange insect shadow moved across the ceiling and into the dark.

She would never tell anybody about that night. Mac thought she had spent the night with her cousin. No one would ever know how she fainted and how she woke up with a strange taste in her mouth, how she left the wooded area, empty of dancers, and wandered into the morning marketplace, so that she could be lost in the crowd until the sun was well up.

Some larvae are fully developed in eggs laid in the fall but hibernate in the egg and do not hatch until spring.

The train screamed, the conductor screamed and everyone lurched. It was finally Jacksonville, N.C. Mac looked anxiously through the window's dust. "Said she'd be here, did she?"

"She'll be here, Mac."

"I hope so. Sure hate to be a outsider."

They climbed down the train steps and began to peer down the platform for her sister. Then Florice saw a Black woman's face rounding the station's corner and realized how much she had missed her sister. "Marie," she called, "Marie Lilly." With the family name Marie started and grinned. The years closed themselves off, and she had to wipe the corner of one eye.

"Girl, don't you know I'm glad to see you." Mac saw Florice really smile for the first time in a month.

The first week was spent discussing what to do when, and trading Creole and North and South Carolina cooking. "Thing to do," said Marie, "is to try for some work here first. And then we'll go for the mills in other places in North Carolina. You good at farmin' Mac?" Mac said he was good at anything that paid. Marie's husband was gone for a week at the time, working fishing boats there on the coast. Mac worried that with Rebecca Florice already half unhappy with him, being gone a week would put a fast end to it all. He decided to look for farm work—he was used to the land, not water.

The white and Black people on the ferry were as separate as the meat and bread they had packed. They had been persuaded by the Simmonses, friends of Marie's, to take a day off from job hunting near the coast, and go for a picnic on Bear Island. Mac had said slowly, "Well, why not? I ain't findin' no work noway." So, they agreed to spend the night at the Simmonses' after a week of frustrating travel in a rig under the unrelenting North Carolina sun.

The ocean was hidden by a land mass; this sound they were crossing was alive with birds: heavy, fecund, with unseen underwater movement. Marsh grass looked as if it had been carefully combed, and the waters of the sound licked at the ferry in rhythm with the steam motor. The water grass was an old green, old as the world, and occasionally there would be an egret standing as if still hypnotized by some giant primitive mammal. Gulls had come in from the open sea, looking for better pickings. They dipped and sang to the invading ferry. Rebecca saw little of this natural paradise, thinking deeply about her coming conversation with Mac. In her fear of what was to come, she saw safety in making one last try with her husband. But what she knew and didn't say was that she was truly headed for open sea and there was no way to turn the ship around. She started her opening sentence a hundred times, as the boat made its way toward Bear Island and the beach. The chugging stopped suddenly and the ferry sidled up to the dock. "Leavin' at 6:30," the ferryman said. "Last boat leavin' at 6:30." Passengers with bags of lunch, binoculars and swimming gear; children with summer-weary parents; and lovers, planning to find private coves: all started in their carefully plotted directions.

Rebecca and Mac made their way slowly in a hazy light that was almost hypnotic. The path led to the other side of the island where there was nothing left of the world but water. Mac carried a basket and a rain slicker. He said nothing. He had insisted on bringing the slicker so they would have something to sit on, and besides "You never know what storm might come up out of the ocean." Rebecca wore a straw hat that she was glad she had, and a light blue dress that floated in an occasional gust of wind. She had never owned a bathing costume. There was a gold cross around her sun-browned neck. The only tangible thing he had ever given her. The dress was cut rather low for the summer, and the cross glowed and glittered on her breasts, in the sun. In the sandy soil that approached the beach, each step left an imprint. They walked slightly separated from each other. She wiped out Mac's footprints. Her low heels left hollows in the path—full spaces, empty spaces, full spaces, empty spaces—Nothing is full, she thought, because everything is empty. But then the sand would run into the hollow. Nothing is empty . . . she stopped and wiped the sweat off her face with a handkerchief. Mac kept going, anxious to be done with this rather tedious promenade. Why am I thinking riddles now? she thought. It's hot as fire and here I stand in the wilderness thinkin' up riddles. On either side of the road were dark evergreen trees growing thickly. The sun and light soil gave a black-green cast to the trees and Mac thought of what kinds of snakes might be hidden within those dark spaces. He turned and noticed her brief stop. "Will you com'on, gal? Damn! It's hot out here!" A trail of perspiration hit her cross and ran between her breasts dampening the blue dress. She picked up her pace. By the time they heard the ocean, she had decided what she would say to Mac. Rebecca sniffed the future, clinging to the skeleton hands of the past. The skeleton whispered that this was the end of the marriage; but she answered, maybe this sharing would bring them back together.

The sky was neither blue, nor gray, but white. The sun was covered by clouds as they climbed the last sand dune, so they could tolerate the lack of shelter and the ocean breeze made up for no umbrella. Gray and blue water, white sky and sand; they spread the slicker out and ate lunch, and for a while it did indeed seem like old times. Mac laughed at her damp dress and she blushed a little. He dared her to get herself wet, and teased, saying that her drawers would stick to her and would show off her shape. After lunch, she took off her hat and shoes and pulled up her skirts just a little, to wade and get cool. Mac was napping in the sun, and Rebecca walked until she was tired, finding especially beautiful shells. They seemed new, like they might have been there in the beginning of the world. She picked up what was almost half a sand dollar because it somehow seemed right, and placed it in the pocket of her dress with the shells. The whole place had a new feel to it, virginal, but too ripe to be young. Simply untouched, that's all. The world must have been young once, she thought. Must have been new once. But she felt so old, so very, very old, like she had walked through all of time, pulling, pulling at an impossible burden that made her life-weary at twenty-two. She felt the beach was a place ready for something, to be touched, to be fondled, to be brought to the fullness of life, simmering just under the surface. Why am I fighting? she thought. There ain't nothin' to fight. The love I had is gone. I ain't never gon love nobody else like that and all this other stuff is just my crazy head playin' tricks on me is all. So I'll tell him, and we'll go on and find a way to live happy and I'll be normal like everybody else. The ocean called her. Today it would change her name. Florice shivered as she thought of being swallowed up in all that water. Something about the edge of the land had always frightened her just a little. She saw Mac sitting up, looking at her.

She started out bravely, with a confidence born of desperation. "Mac, listen," she said as she sat down, "I got to tell you something." The words rushed out, tumbling in a frightened heap on the sand. "I was crazy this last month. I was really crazy. I know you been thinking something was really wrong with me and I guess you had a right. I had a vision, Mac. Some folks would say I was touched or fixed, back home, I know. But really, Mac, I was sittin' by the fire and I coulda sworn I heard a voice say I was supposed to heal folks and give my life for God and all, and I just didn't know what to do, Mac, I just didn't know what to do, so I stopped talkin' to you or anybody else, Mac, and I just been talkin' to God and I just couldn't stand for you to touch me, I was just so scared and . . ." Florice looked up at Mac and she knew immediately she had made the last mistake the marriage could hold.

"You what, girl? You talked to God?" Mac grabbed her arm and left a bruise mark from his thumb. "How you come . . . how you come to take me for dumb! I know what you been doin'!" The rage was climbin' up his legs and when it reached his hands, she knew she would be in danger unless she could talk his anger back to that small lump where it had hidden for so many months.

"What I been doin', then? What? You think it's some man?"

He laughed, roughly. "Naw, not some man, some half a man; the kind that wears dresses to church!" He jerked her forward, still sitting on the sand, still holding her arm. She kept herself from saying it hurt, because she knew he would like that and that it would feed his anger.

"Mac, you got it wrong, you got it wrong! Father Canty

was helpin' me. Helpin' me understand what was goin' on
inside me.''

''I know what was goin' on inside you, girl, and it didn't
have nothin' to do with God or no church, or no healin'. You
crazy, bitch. I always thought you was strange. Mixin' all
that shit up. God, and healin', and your *insides*. You crazy!''
He had finally let her go and was standing over her, desperate
with her, with his love for her, and with himself. ''You, heal
somebody? Folks either get well or they die. That's all there
is to that, and nothin' nobody can do about it! Least of all
you!''

''Mac, there's somethin' else; Mac, there's somethin' in
me that won't let go, that won't leave me alone, never. Mac,
I been prayin', tryin' to hide deep down in myself but it's no
help for it. It comes risin' up like that wave out there, moves
me to do somethin' different, to help make folks feel better,
to love folks so I could cry and cry, and I can't say no to
that—that's God, Mac, that's got to be God.'' Florice knew
as she talked that she was hearing her own answer and lookin'
at the future full in the face. It set the hairs straight up on her
arms. So there was no escape, there was no going back. The
waters would swell and die and swell and die and swell again
and finally there was no pushing them back to stay. Her eyes
were wet with understanding; she was nodding her head and
rocking back and forth and Mac's anger brought her no fear.
She had left him for God, and he would never never accept
that, though he really knew that Theodore had only been her
dream. ''Mac, I never did anything; I never gave him nothin'.
He was real religious, Mac; he wouldn't . . . touch me.''
She had whispered those last words, because they still
brought up too much out of that deep well for her to bear.
She looked up; he was facing the ocean, unable to look at
her. She hurt for him, for them all. He started walking, then
running, as fast as the sun would allow. He turned, screaming, frightened, wrestling with this enormous, confused, im-
potence.

''. . . it was some god, it was some god you were in bed
with, not that half-white motherfucker with the backwards
collar! Not the candles you loved, not that stinkin' incense,

not even that Christ on the cross, but some god!'' She could see his mouth moving in the waves, his beautiful hurt eyes crashing between each word. She wondered, did she really do that? And how do you atone for that and would anyone ever understand her, her half-white priest even? She could still hear his voice fighting the enormity of the ocean; it would be with her a long time. The last time she ever saw him, he had fallen, trying to climb a sand dune, falling down, running again wildly. She watched him get smaller and smaller and finally he was out of sight. How would she get off the island now? The sea gulls whined; she understood, and wrapped herself up for the night in the slicker Mac had left behind.

As a caterpillar grows it sheds its skin, or molts. This permits another period of growth.

1915–1919

The Simmonses were scandalized, but very giving. They asked almost no questions when she said Mac had run off, just insisted that she take those shoes off, rest her feet, and spend the night, though they did think she was a strange woman because she showed no signs of weeping, and having heard once they hadn't seen him, she didn't bring his name up again. Joe Simmons said, more'n likely she'd break down later, like some folks held it in when they had a death. Marnie Simmons kept shaking her head and saying, what a shame, what a shame; shame. Joe offered to take Florice back to Marie's and insisted, when she said she could manage with the horse and wagon they had brought.

So the thing was done. Marie enfolded her sister and was more than a little glad she'd be staying for a while.

Florice was floating free, but she was alone in all that space. She kept remembering there was some reason she should be grieving, and then his eyes would come back, and his voice, screaming about the half-white preacher. But he was as far away as his voice in the waves, and often at night she'd pray for him, all the time feeling guilty about being free and not feeling, not being connected to him anymore. For a while they'd asked around town after him but he seemed to have vanished. Plukey White said aloud, maybe that fella just might have done himself in, but *nobody* would come out and say it to Marie, and everybody knew Plukey was half-cocked.

She had brought the seeds with her from New Orleans, intending to replant her herb garden wherever they ended up staying. Now, a whole year later, she unpacked them carefully, one packet at a time. She was uncommonly good with plants. Anything would grow in Louisiana, she used to say, throwing off any compliments about her lush garden. Can't help but grow here, bein' hot and wet all the time. But others knew that there was something about her garden that was special. Except no seed's ever grown in my own belly, she thought. There was always a chance, but she was almost afraid to form the words in her mind; there was always a chance that there would be another man and another home. So she formed the images instead. Of herself and a man whom she always saw as very dark and all smiles, and of a small person. She always saw only the back of his head, only the back of a small head and a thin back, and it worried her to have the picture inside her. But she kept it there on the attic floor of her thoughts because of what it might mean. For a whole year, since Mac ran away, she had seen herself and the man, and the back of the small head. It was time to plant; time to grow new plants and time to admit that the emptiness of what had been was over.

Rebecca laid them out carefully on her sister's dresser scarf, a packet from each of the plants down home—fennel seed, thyme, allspice, basil, rosemary, mace, nutmeg, mint, parsley, and sweet false chamomile. She had listened carefully for a week and she knew that today she should do her planting. On the right side of Marie's small house, three feet away from the window, she carefully dug the first row of earth. "Yes, that's right," she said. This close to the sea, soil was sandy, loose. Rebecca added fertilizer from a bucket and mixed carefully. Moistened the soil mixture with just half a bucket of water, nodded her head as if she understood, and laid in her herb garden just below the surface of the earth. Where she was kneeling, her deep pink dress showed the earth marks. She brushed, but it smeared. That was fine, she thought, wouldn't matter. No man anymore to be prettyin' up for anyway. She looked up at the hot North Carolina sky, said thank you aloud and turned to go up the weather-beaten steps. Marie Lilly had been starin' out the front door for a few minutes. "Girl, the sun done gone to your head. Who you talkin' to out there?" Rebecca looked at her sister, started to say something, but changed her mind. She had a way of knowing what folks were ready to hear. "Don't you never mind, Marie Lilly," she said. "I got just as much sense as I always had. Ain't met the man yet, can drive me crazy," and thought to herself, I hope I don't regret sayin' that.

"Life does turn itself roun' to meet you," said Marie.

They had mint tea three weeks later and Marie forgot about her sister talking to herself and told all her church friends how her sister grew the prettiest herb garden she had ever seen and grew plants she never heard of. Basil and allspice to beat the band. One rainy Sunday after services, Marie introduced Rebecca to Alice—a very black woman, short, stocky, and powerful. She had a deep voice and the children in Jacksonville often told secret jokes about Alice Wine's "man's voice." They didn't dare mention it to their parents. Tommy Grant said she got that voice from drinkin' wine 'cause her name *was* Wine, and his mother had slapped him halfway across the room. For more than a year, Rebecca had made no friends aside from her sister, and she finally knew that it wasn't making sense to separate herself from the world because she was a woman alone and a woman in pain. Marie said, "Rebecca, this here's Alice, Alice Wine." She looked straight into Alice's eyes and saw a space she knew about. Rebecca had been in those secret and dark caves, wearing black under her pink and yellow and blue frocks. She knew those caves well, every small hole full of dark water, every sudden drop of the hard stone floor, every narrow precipice where you would lose your footing if you felt your attention wander for an instant, and every fluttering bat that she had crossed her hands over her head and tried to hide from. She had been in those caves too long to go on and there was that scratchin' in her stomach. She took Alice's hand. "Nice morning." It was said more as a statement than a question. Marie looked kind of strange and said, "It's rainin', Florice." And Alice just smiled and shook her head.

She was from sea island stock and though her people had seen that she learned to talk like folks on the mainland, Alice still knew the Gullah, and still had the accent. "Oha now Florice, oha now gurl, it's coming up a storm," she would warn in her low voice. Alice always knew when it was going to storm, half by being born on a sea island, and half by being Alice.

Florice had found work as a cook and baby-sitter, and Alice was a housekeeper. They were live-in help (though Marie protested Florice's moving away from her), and were within walking distance of each other's jobs. One day a week, they didn't have to work and sleep in someone else's home; often they ended up at Marie's house sharing in meals and talk. It was 1919 and it was a terrible time to be Black. They kept hearing things about riots in the North, and Black boys being killed in the streets. The summer was a heavy wet covering weighing on their eyes; heat was so present you had to carry it, like taking your bed covering with you wherever you went. Alice and Florice sat on the front porch sipping chamomile tea from Florice's herb garden and being silent. Florice's head had hurt most of the day. Jude and Marie had gone in for the night. Somewhere from a long distance they began to hear a growl of sound. Except for the deep heat, and the fact that most everybody had given up trying to do anything but get some sleep before tomorrow's sun hit, they would not have heard it, but they would have known. Florice had seen it that afternoon, white, on a horse with fire where its eyes should be. She had seen it covering the town, throwin' its gray smell over them all, and wrappin' up Jacksonville in a shroud. Alice knew there was a reason for Florice's headache. The short black hair on her neck curled up tighter with the heat of the night.

The growl at the back of their heads stayed where it was. They heard shrill nips of dogs high in the air, and the sky was a faint pink over black. Alice counted each blink of Florice's eyes. She had stopped rocking and Alice knew Florice was listening, listening. And so Alice sat, strangely content with her own horror. It comforted, like knowing when you are finally lost in the woods and you sit down under a tree and wait for God to tell you which way is out. They sat together in the dark, through the hour it must have taken to kill. And when they both knew it was over, Florice came back to the world and they rose to go in the house, to lock the doors and to join the sleepless night of those who guarded what they had in terror, and those who grieved that their God had once again seen fit to remind them what faith is.

Somewhere that morning there was a family quietly screaming, a family which had long ago forgotten that there was a world outside blood, fire, and ripping fear. They knew only the twenty-eight square feet of their shotgun house and they knew only, only, the truth of blowing fear. The wind-burn of rape and death.

She packed up some liquor Marie said Jude had been saving since January for next Christmas, and some pork and greens and a chicken. And she set out, following her mind like a map.

Alice would come. She would not be put off. They walked down the dirt path. Florice stumbled on a stone but she righted herself, quickly. Alice was carrying things to eat. It was Sunday, their time off. They bit their lips: there had been enough tears shed already. There it was. They had not let anybody in. They had not gone to claim the boy's burnt body. They had not moved for twelve hours. The house carried its sorrow and fear on props, like many houses born by the South; it sagged on one side. There were no windows, a closed front door, and a closed back door.

Florice breathed in once, and out once. She walked up the three steps and knocked. There was no answer. Alice stood on the ground before the steps. "Miz Peabody?" A fly was walking over a large white K that had been painted on the front door. "Miz Peabody, hello? We just thought y'all could stand a little company? It's Rebecca Florice and Alice out here." She tried the door.

Someone had quietly gotten up and unlocked it while she was talking. It creaked open just a little. Alice saw a fear that was deeper than midnight blue on the faces of three women, two young ones, and an older woman. They were on the floor in a corner, one still in a spot which smelled of urine let loose during last night's kidnapping. The faces were lost. This pain was not familiar. This wilderness blinded. They had had a brother. They had had a father. Lost in a silent whirl of ghosts snatching at their clothes, their private spaces violated, their precious hidden selves blown through with rasping death. They had had a father; they had known a son, brother, husband. Alice and Florice gently lifted the women from the filth on the floor. "Come on now, y'all, let's see here, let's see." Florice, talking mostly to keep herself moving, guided them to a back room where there were five pallets and laid each of them back down. Florice washed bodies; Alice warmed food and finally the time came when they could let go of their fear and let sorrow in.

The friends walked home that night softly talking of how it had happened again and Oh Lord when would it end and while Florice climbed the steps to Marie's porch her legs started trembling. She went to put on the kettle and couldn't lift it. Marie took it out of her hands and stirred up the wood stove's fire. She set the kettle on the burner and gently pushed Florice into a chair. To Marie, Florice looked very young in the lamplight. She had seen into that horrible ritual of sacrifice, she had stood next to it; she had washed away its blood and this had stripped her sister of all but the faintest veneer of adulthood, and in the face of hell she was a child, but a child come through to the other side. Marie knew what she saw on her sister's face, and was frightened for her. "They, they, they cut . . . cut . . . the body. . . ." Florice stammered. When she dropped her teacup, Jude took her arm and guided her to bed without a word.

> *Both butterflies and moths emerge with soft, limp, moist wings which slowly expand as fluids are pumped through the veins. Later the veins harden, providing a rigid support for the wing membrane.*

1923

Jude was bound to leave Jacksonville. He had been saving up, piecing pennies together for years to get out of this place where Black life, he said, "wunt worth a dime, a dime." The Brazletons were leaving and they had a truck that could carry both him and Marie and they could manage on what they had saved. Marie looked teary for weeks before they were due to leave. What would Florice do without them? She knew what a woman alone faced. Living out her days in some white woman's house, taking care of some white woman's children, and keeping quiet every time somebody said something about niggers, or worse, did something. And what was even worse, maybe never havin' a family again, a family of her own.

She heard Jude fussin' in the kitchen with Henry Brazleton. "It's Detroit, man, it's Detroit! They tell me that's where we oughta go." Henry opened his mouth. "Naw, man, wait a minute; wait just a damn minute. Chicago is guaranteed, you say? Guaranteed! Don't everybody know, nothing is guaranteed to no nigger?"

"Naw man, you know what I mean," said Henry. "They got meat packin' there. You got to feed folks, right? And white folks are gonna eat their steak ain't they? So we goin' to someplace where there ain't gonna be no chance of runnin' out, you know what I mean?"

"Listen man, these new cars they gon build, this is the comin' thing, man."

Marie shook her head. It sure didn't matter to her. She didn't know nobody up there noways, and it was sure to be lonely for her, always was for women wherever they went. She was thankful for Emma Brazleton, and her brother who was already in Chicago. Maybe that's where they should go 'cause they'd know somebody; anybody'd be better'n nobody.

She heard Henry's glass of home brew being thumped on the table. "You *got* to *go*, where the *work* is, man, not where it gon be." Between the two of them and that brew they'd be sure to end up in Texas, Marie thought. She kept packing and wondered since they were the ones wanted to go so bad, why was she doin' all the work?

Henry finally won out and their destination was Chicago. Marie was more worried about leaving her sister than she was about going to such a big place. She knew some city life from a New Orleans childhood. She could handle that. But could Rebecca handle being alone?

They were almost ready. Friday came and Rebecca came in at 6:30 as usual with Alice. "Y'all, we got somethin' to tell you." She looked determined and decided. "Alice Wine and me, we are leaving this place. We can get a train out tomorrow for Greensboro and we're goin'."

Marie looked at her sister, wide-eyed. She was always headstrong. No sense in asking her if she was certain because Marie knew if she wasn't certain, Rebecca Florice wouldn't have announced she was leaving.

"Y'all got jobs?" said Jude. He was the only one in the group not a little afraid of his sister-in-law.

Alice volunteered, "It's a Negro college there. They always needin' folks to cook and such. Be nice to work for our people for a change."

"Well, I'll be," said Jude, "go *on*. Y'all some brazen huzzies, and I just wish you the *best*. Listen, Henry, can we fit these ladies and a baby in the truck? Save y'all some train fare and all."

Florice smiled. Jude had been a strong tree for her since Mac had run off. She would miss him. "Jude, don't you worry none. Henry's got three younguns to fit in the back of that truck and that's enough."

Marie put her arm around her sister, and walked her out onto the porch. They would never have another time quite like the last eight years. Marie stared straight ahead, her hand lightly resting on Rebecca's shoulder. "You take care of yourself, baby sister." Rebecca Florice nodded.

"Feels right, Marie, like I'm going where I'm supposed to be."

"Then that's what you supposed to do. You got a good friend in Alice. That's good. God looks after his children." It was getting dark. A breeze ruffled the pines and brought the faint scent of mint and thyme from the herb garden. What they didn't say was what they said.

1928

The school was mostly dirt and three buildings. There was a kitchen and a dining room, a classroom or two, and a dormitory for girls. Boys had to find places in town to sleep. Rebecca and Alice cooked for the whole school of fifty students and three teachers and cleaned the kitchen and dining rooms. All the students had "duty work," so Alice and Rebecca had some help. Dr. Benedict, the principal, had found rooms for them in a place for single ladies.

One cold evening, Rebecca decided to share her things with Alice. She took an old corset box down from the closet shelf. "The Gentle Woman's Helpers Co." was printed on the side.

Alice was reading the Bible.

"Looka here, gurl," said Florice.

"Hm?" She looked up from her reading. It was really very chilly and Alice had wrapped up in her quilt. "What you laughin' at?" she said in her island accent.

"You, sittin' there like a Indian or something."

"Rather be funny lookin' than cold. Ooh gurl, always did hate to be cold. What chu got there?"

"This is my special box. All these things come from somewhere I been, you see."

"Go 'long, gurl. That looks like some hoodoo to me. Go 'long, gurl. I know that stuff from the old home place. Don't you be doin' no funny stuff roun' here now."

Florice let out one of her rare, bell-like laughs. It was full laughter, rich with being alive. Alice was shaking her head. "No suh, gurl, no suh." Florice laughed again and Alice was finding it impossible not to join her friend's delight.

A woman, in her thirties, and a woman in her forties were full of sun and tipping over the cup to let the joy run out. Alice's quilt fell on the floor and she lost her place in the Scripture, but she no longer felt cold. "Oh gurl, when have I laughed like that!" She leaned back in her rocking chair, and looked out into the cold night. She rocked once or twice and spoke slowly in her clipped speech. Though the words came out fast, there were many long pauses between them. "Used to be an old woman . . . a root woman you know, Florice" . . . Alice took a breath . . . "and we little uns be 'fraid to go near her place . . . and one time she fixed a gurl, so they said . . . and we's certain she drown herself 'cause dat woman . . . they told us chillun she carried the gurl's hair in her pocket . . . and she threw it into the runnin' water, and the next day, the gurl run wild, tearin' up folks' flowers and rollin' on the ground . . . and den she run off . . . and they done found hur, Florice . . . dat night as the sun go down, in dat runnin' stream, way down the way . . . drowned to death."

They were both silent for a minute. Alice peered over into the box. There were several packets which Alice knew by the smell were herbs and herb seeds. Rosemary and mint, sweet false chamomile, five-fingers grass, scallop and jopo holy root. She saw a half sand dollar, several other shells, an old piece of clapboard wood, some pressed flowers, and, most miraculous of all, a pressed butterfly and a dead scarab beetle. Something in Alice was satisfied just to look. She was privileged. She had seen a hidden room, a secret passageway. It was not necessary to ask any questions. Love is a rest, in space. The chair squeaked. The French clock ticked. Florice put the top on her box and put it back under her extra blankets.

1929

She turned over and was suddenly awake, not sure she heard someone, but something had startled her awake and she lay silent, listening. There was a knock. Downstairs. Sounded like the back door. Must have been one of the girls in trouble of some kind. She smoothed her hair down a little and hurried to get into her robe on the way down the steps. The thought that it might be Eadie having another one of her hysterical fits was depressing. As the knock became more urgent, she peered out through the glass. There were only three women living in the house right now. She calculated where her biggest butcher knife was and opened the inside storm door.

"I heard you could do it," he said, through the screen. She was thinking faster than she wanted to, so she just nodded so as not to interrupt her thought. "I heard you could make people well."

"Uh . . . who says such things?" She almost said it to herself. Well, there it was, out; and once out, that kind of gossip never died, except by the death of its main victim, and then maybe not. She was in it now, she thought, God help me. She took her gaze off the stranger's watery eyes. He had not even heard her, convinced as he was that she was either angel or devil and possessed of his own passion to see for himself.

"I dreamed you could do it. I been watchin' you a long time walkin' back and forth up there at the school and first I just think you awful purty and then I knowed you could do it. You waz in mah dream. I saw you pickin' them plants an things. I thought maybe you'se a witch but you come tuh me in a dream and I knows it's for real. God touches those that's got the power, mum. Ah kin see it in yo' eyes, don't you know. Ah kin see it. Some'm us sees it, and some'm us does it, and you, does it. Ah know.''

She was wary and nervous as she opened the screen door. This was like marriage, either the beginning of freedom or slavery. Out of the corner of her eye, she saw sores blistering on the left side of his mouth, and sighed.

"Are you thirsty or hungry, sir, and may I call you by name?'' The man was hungry and very dirty. He asked to wash his hands. Florice indicated the sink and turned to the ice box to get some cold chicken. She had to turn her back to him to get some bread out of the window box hooked on the outside of the kitchen window. She slid the window open and reached for the bread, glancing out at the sleeping houses up and down the street. It was 1:30 A.M. The slamming window shot a burst of cold air across her face. He sat down at the kitchen table, his greasy overalls hiding how very thin his body was. He ate in silence. Florice leaned on the counter, trying to appear casual. She held her coffee with one hand and pulled her chenille robe closer. The heat was off for the night.

Whether the man was Indian or white, you couldn't tell. He had straight black hair and skin like the desert floor in the winter. He didn't smell of alcohol, only of many days' sweat. Florice asked a second time, "What did you say you wanted here?'' Hoping against hope that he was really only hungry.

"These sores, ma'am, I wonder if you could just pray over 'em a leetle bit? I done repented, and I's been born again, and I still ain't well a'tall. I ain't ever been to no doctor an I ain't gonna start now. Maybe I just ain't no good.''

Florice closed her eyes and sighed. She remembered the Light in her hands. Her senses told her that he had syphilis and her common sense told her that she should send him away, but something held her there. He so clearly believed she could do it. She moved toward him and put her coffee on the table. His smell reminded her of pig farms back in New Orleans.

"Before I do this, you must promise me not to tell anyone. And if I help you, you must promise me not to tell anyone I did it. I don't know how it works, I don't know if I can really help you at all, but since you are here, I'll try." He nodded. His eyes were weak and she knew he would die if she didn't at least make an effort. She leaned over him and put her hands on the sores.

"It's right warm," he said. "I feel it gettin' right warm." She took her hands down. "What is your name?" she said. "I need your name."

"It's Ralph, ma'am, it's Ralph."

"I'll pray for you Ralph," she said.

"But that's all you got to do?"

"Yes, Ralph, that's all. You go 'long now."

"I shore do thank you, ma'am, I shore do. I'll pray for you, too, ma'am. Them sores, they feel better already. I won't tell nobody, I swear I won't. I swear I won't. God bless you, ma'am, God bless you."

She almost had to push him out of the door, and she locked it with relief, and threw his milk glass in the trash can. Ralph kept his word. It would be almost ten years before she laid hands on anyone else. She would be too busy learning that love never comes to call without its twin.

1930

She met his eyes when he met the congregation. There was never any question of maybe for Florice. When she saw a man, either she did or she didn't. Either she would or she wouldn't, not ever. This was not love, or so she thought, this was just pure wanton lusting after a man. No point in being a silly woman. She'd just have to control it. She tried not to let him know, but trying is, of course, admitting to failure, and not many men had the good sense to look lust in the eye and turn it down.

The first failure came after the Wednesday night supper. There had been much eating and much praying and also much laughter. Florice found herself alone in the church kitchen, putting the finishing touches on the cleaning up.

"Left you alone, did they? Could you use some help?" He took the broom gently from her reluctant hands.

"Why, no, Reverend, you let me do that. You must have things to do."

"Nothin' better'n helpin' a pretty lady, I'd say. Let's see, it's Miss Rebecca, right?"

"Yes sir." She was looking at some sparkling clean dishes, wishing they were still covered with dinner's crust.

"So how did you enjoy the supper?" He didn't wait for an answer. "I intend to have these once a week. I think they might bring us together, don't you?"

She who was never at a loss for an answer, who was a symbol of self-control and strength, stuttered and looked for a doorway, but it had disappeared. "I said, I think they will bring us together, don't you think?" He was looking much too far into her, much too directly at her face.

"Yes, Reverend. Excuse me, Rev, please."

Well, girl, you are just old enough to know better, she said to herself. Thirty-seven years old and flittin' around like a young firefly. She kicked at a stone on the sidewalk on her way home.

Robert Brown put the broom up and turned out the lights. He went to the back of the church, opened the door to his office, and began the sermon for Sunday. The scripture reference was Corinthians 1:13.

1932

Florice heard a knock on the back door of the dining room. She put down her knife and called out to Alice, "Be right back."

Wiping the sliced cabbage off her hands onto her apron, she opened the door. "Yes?"

" 'Scuse me, honey, but my feet are just painin' me and I was wondering if y'all could spare a little glass of somethin' cool and a chair? I figured you just might be able to tell me if y'all had seen somebody I'm lookin' for? I'm missing a Mr. Joseph T. J. Jones, and I know y'all hires folks from time to time?" By this time she was in the door and looking Florice up and down and looking the dining room up and down and talking all at the same time.

"Won't you come on back here, and we'll see about some iced tea for you."

"Thank you, honey; I was just sayin' the other day, folks thinks y'all uppity over here at the college, and I says y'all are wrong, you're just as wrong, and I says cause I just know, if I went over there and asked for somethin', they'd give it to me. My name's Selma Martin, honey, you just call me Selma, and your name?"

"Rebecca. I believe we have some tea here left from yesterday. Now what can I help you with?"

Alice, steadily frying chicken, strained over the cracking, popping grease to hear the conversation and Selma was very aware of her presence, but was waiting to see if Alice would be "uppity" or if she would come over and say who she was. Alice decided it wasn't worth it to ignore the lady, even though she knew Dr. Benedict would think this a little irregular, and would tell them he couldn't be giving out free drinks to stray people from the neighborhood.

"Hey," she said, "Alice Wine."

"How do, honey. Real pleased to meet y'all. Now where was I? Oh yes, a Mr. Joseph T. J. Jones—y'all heard anything at all about him? You know these nigger men." Florice flinched ever so slightly. "You just can't depend on 'em to do nothin' but run out on your ass! Well, anyway, he was payin' me you know, for doin' him a little favor and he just up and run out and took some of my money, and this was maybe a year ago you know. So I thought it's about time he's due to come back and look for some easy money 'cause he'll be back sooner or later. So since it's 'bout time he ran out of money, I thought he just might be knockin' on y'all's door for trash collectin' or yard workin' or somethin'. And if y'all see him I'd 'preciate y'all tellin' me."

Florice and Alice heard all this, knowing it may or may not have been true, and knowing the real reason she came in was to see what the school was like up on that hill. And somehow, that was all right with them. They were all on the outside of one thing or another.

Selma's hair was in its usual treetop state and she had on a pair of old houseshoes. Alice wondered if she needed work. And was Joseph T. J. Jones really a paying customer or was she just wanting him back 'cause half a man was supposed to be better'n none? She had no idea what the truth was. "Selma, if you'd like, gurl, I can ask the Dr. Benedict if there's any work here." She didn't really expect the answer she got.

"Why, that'd be very nice of you, honey. That would be right nice." She placed her tea glass on the large table, very slowly. It looked like this interview was about over; Selma couldn't think of anything more to say so she rose.

"I sho do thank y'all. I sho do. I can find my way out. Bye now."

Florice watched her back go through the door. "Now Miss Alice, what you gone and done?" she said.

"Nothin', gal. Just you don't mind. I'll see to it." Alice

kept on frying chicken. Florice just shook her head at her friend's good-hearted generosity.

The next Monday morning, Florice saw Selma in a new housedress on campus. "Why, hello, Selma, how've you been?" She was halfway worried that if she stopped to speak she'd be late to work.

"Girl," said Selma, she was now sure of herself, feeling on a par with Alice and Florice; this was her campus now. "Dr. Benedict, he's just the nicest man for a college 'fessor man you know, and he give me a job cleanin' in his own house, and, girl, that is a fine house, you hear me? You know they got china and stuff like *white* folks got and 'course I think sometime he think he white, don't you?" Florice didn't answer. "Well, I'll be seeing y'all real soon cause I eats lunch in the dining hall, I think." She bounced off with her hair flying; Alice thought, Dr. Benedict's wife would soon have to deal with that hair. She knew how Mrs. Benedict "expected her help to look." She had heard that phrase when she was hired.

1934

Jessie was a fine lady. There was no question about it. A good woman who would stick with you through thick and thin. He took out his handkerchief and cleaned his reading glasses. She took being a mother seriously and enjoyed it. At least he thought she enjoyed it. The kids were reasonably happy and not unreasonably unruly, for preacher's kids. Jessie had made a home for them in the parsonage. That wasn't easy in a pre-furnished old place where the church deacons had decided what would or wouldn't be bought, and what was "suitable" for a preacher's house. The congregation loved her and she suited the job of preacher's wife so well it was as if she had taken lessons. She always knew what to wear, she always knew what to say, she always knew what to do. Robert sighed, that Saturday afternoon, sitting over his sermon notes. He couldn't understand what was wrong with him. How could he be looking at another woman at this time of life? And after all Jessie had sacrificed and given up for him? There was no excuse, but there was nowhere to run, either. Everywhere he turned he met his fascination for her. He could blame it on the devil, but he never really believed in such things, no matter what he told the church on Sunday mornings, and there was one thing he did know; he knew the difference between the devil and Robert Brown and it was painfully clear to him that this desire belonged to Robert Brown. She carried a fire inside her that he saw every time she moved. She lived: if she did nothing else, she lived. And he wanted the fire in a way he couldn't understand. He'd heard people say she was strange and could "fix" you, but he'd never paid any attention to such gossip. Jessie dropped

a lid in the kitchen. He shook his head, and forced himself
to get back to work, noticing the clock said 3:30 already and
she would be calling him to dinner at 5:30 sharp as she always did. She was real proud that he never had to wait for
his dinner and that the children were always present and on
time. She would have the boiled potatoes and Swiss steak
she had every Saturday. He swallowed, and flipped the pages
of his Bible quietly. Noticing, but not noticing, the fresh
flower on his desk. Somewhere inside himself, he had just
made the decision that would change his life. Knowing he
was going to have steak and potatoes had pushed a button he
had been avoiding for four years. Jessie came tiptoeing up
to the desk and tapped him on the shoulder at 5:30. He kissed
her on the cheek and really enjoyed his dinner for the first
time in months. He was going to gamble, and he was laying
for the highest stakes a man could risk.

"Take therefore no thought for the morrow," he preached
Sunday, "sufficient unto the day is the evil thereof." He
entitled his sermon "Gambling for God" and people said it
was the finest sermon he had ever preached. At least three
people got happy and Miss Althenia Taylor joined the church,
which was a surprise to everybody since she had been holding out for years.

* * *

There would be no disturbance of the careful building that
was their marriage. He would do it expertly, carefully and
secretly. She was beautiful, but that wasn't really it. He told
himself he could be forgiven for wanting to live, and he had
been so good for so long. She wanted him, and she loved
him.

The reddish brown hair on her arms registered his energy.
She had felt him all day, brushing against her lightly, a ghost
whose desire was exciting and frightening. What could be
the end of it? She had loved him for four years, in spite of
the rules or any of the rest of it. A little cleaning, a little
cooking, she paced most of the day Monday. Late afternoon.
He rang the doorbell.

Some reason for coming. To explain the new money-raising project, to ask support of the women of the church, to see her.

To see her. To touch her hair. To see her alone. To put his arm around her waist, and pull her in, and wonder why this couldn't be his, why it had to be wrong like this.

They were in the eye of the storm and the only way to safety was through the water's fury. The wind at their hearts made a great deal of noise.

1935

He was what they called a nice young man. Except he had been North for too long and forgot his home trainin'. That Monday morning his desperation was clear, for anybody who had eyes to see. Robert was just arriving at the church and met Joe in the parking lot. After good mornings and questions, they sat in the office together while Joe outlined what he had been through, and asked Robert Brown for advice. Robert hesitated. This was difficult and dangerous. Also, he felt it was hopeless. A nineteen-year-old Black boy wanting a machine job in the mill. There was no way. Even if he had done it in Youngstown, Ohio. There was no way he would ever break through, and Robert felt frightened for him and for himself.

He started out answering, knowing his response would be no response at all, feeling anger at himself, and strangely, at Joe and feeling totally inadequate.

"Just what do you think I can do, son? There's no union; there's no protection. What do you think I can do?" Joe said something hopeless about the influence of the church. Robert fingered his lapel and glanced at the cross on his desk. "Son, you're talking about a million-dollar business, and all the power white men have. You're talking about puttin' yourself and anyone who helps you in danger; about the Klan and lynching. That's what you're talking about. Now you go on out and find you some kinda job where you can bring home enough to take care 'a your mama. That's what I think you oughta do. I'll pray over it and I'll pray for you." He scraped his chair as a signal the interview was over, and extended his hand. Joe's hand was trembling, and he just barely touched Robert as he turned to go.

Tuesday they were saying he had been beat, but nobody knew for sure. Robert knew only too well what had happened. Joe had stood in line for two hours and when he got to the foreman, he had asked politely for a job, and the white foreman had looked up from his desk and said, "Well, we have a place here for a boy to clean up the latrine and sweep up the trash and clean out the bins. You reckon you could do that?" And Joe had said he was a machine operator back in Ohio and the cracker had laughed real loud and said, "Well, now, I never knew a nigger boy could operate a machine," and said "You better take that back to Ohio, boy." And Joe had slammed the door on his way out and gone to the colored side of town. And the colored CIO chairman had said, "Ain't no colored man gonna get no machine job down here. What chu come back down here for? Welcome home." And he had laughed too—and then he had come to Robert and said he came south 'cause his mama was sick and what was he gonna do, and Robert had said he'd pray over it and now Joe Gray was in jail for assault and lucky to be alive because he'd pushed a white man on the street and times were hard.

Times were hard. Everybody was scraping pennies, and everybody knew there wasn't much to go around. There had been just so many jobs available and no colored were going to be hired when whites weren't eating regularly. Robert walked quietly over to the church office and sat for a long time wondering what he should do. He had been called into the mayor's office and asked to help "quiet things down" in his church. There had been a terrible riot up in Harlem just the week before. Folks had read about it and heard about it on the radio. The papers were full of how many Negro boys were looting and how these unruly mobs of Blacks caused death and destruction in the fair city of New York all over some wild criminal of fifteen years old who had stolen a knife to commit a terrible and unspeakable crime. Robert was told he could quiet our Negro citizens; he was told he could preach about patience and how folks should "wait on the Lord." He sat down heavily in his chair. He had just come from the jail. Joe was not "up to visitors," they said, and Robert had been told he was in the infirmary. He tapped his pencil nervously in the heavy silence and bowed his head. It had been a long time since he had believed in his own prayers. Folks were upset all over town. Selma was full of stories of fear and afraid to take the bus to town.

Florice and Alice remembered the lynching they had lived through in 1919 and shuddered. The girls at the college were told to be extra careful and curfew was moved up to 8:00 P.M. That night they had planned a little supper with June Peters and her sister, friends from the church. Alice had made gumbo and Florice was making cornbread when the doorbell rang. "Girl," June started, "we came early. Things are bad. You might have us overnight, because we hear the Klan has put out a warning." Florice shook cornmeal off her hands, wiped them, and took their coats. She was glad to see them, but her mind was on Robert. "We'll be fine," she said. He had said something about an NAACP meeting, and he had preached Sunday, a sermon she had not known he could preach—about courage and faith in hard times and he had said that Joe Gray was innocent and that if he did die, the whole town would know who to blame. Right out in the pulpit! It was wonderful, but it worried her more than a little. Where was he going, and where would he end up? Where would they both end up?

Despite the cloud of danger around them, they enjoyed the food and gossip. About 8:00 the doorbell rang. It was Mr. Newell, the college maintenance man. "Ma'am, Miss Florice, I'm just checkin' the rounds. Dr. Benedict he asked me to see was everybody in and all right, cause y'all know what happened has folks a little nervous." He looked over his shoulder and lowered his voice. "Ma'am, that boy Joe? Well, he died tonight and word's not out yet, but you know, just keep your door locked, ma'am." She shut the door quietly. That was it. She had to call Robert, wife or no wife. Florice went straight to the kitchen phone without going back into the living room. His number. His wife. She knew. She didn't dare ask where he was. She didn't dare say they were in danger. She did say that Mrs. Brown and the children were

welcome to come over for a while until the night was over.
Mrs. Jessie Brown thanked her politely and hung up.

"We done heard," Alice said as she walked back to the
living room. "The boy is dead." They all sat, stunned as if
waiting for God's next move. June and Martha decided to
spend the night. It was now dark. They thought of many
things to say to each other and didn't. "That poor mother,"
June finally said. "My Bernard will be that age soon. He's
in California now with his aunt." Alice suggested Chinese
checkers and so they played that for a while, as if their lives
depended on where the marbles fell. And then there was
Monopoly, and ice cream and cake, and then the phone rang.
Alice said, "I'll get it" very firmly and walked to the phone.
Her oxford heels fell heavily, shaking the floor a little. It was
Selma. Florice heard her say—"burning? What about the
pastor's house?" "What about the family?" Florice heard
herself asking, and she heard Alice say from far away, "They
say it was a warnin'. They OK. They OK. Just night riders
go by . . . burn a cross in the yard." Alice got sheets out for
their guests. They turned out the lights and went to bed,
quickly.

This was not Harlem. There were not as many hungry
people here, there were not as many jobless. But there were
some broken windows that night, and some small knots of
Black men standing on Market St. in coveralls, some chewing on tobacco, some with sticks in their hands, and they
argued about what should be done and what shouldn't be
done, nervously itching to do . . . something. Just something. And there were small knots of white men on the edge
of town in coveralls with tobacco stains, nervously watching
and arguing about what should be done and what shouldn't
be done about that uppity nigger who had got what he deserved in jail and whose preacher had come to the jail and
complained about not being able to see him. There was a
rumor that he had been talkin' to the big boys downtown,
complainin', that he had tried to get in to see the mayor even.
They had taught him a lesson tonight—taught all them niggers a lesson. Next time wouldn't be no cross burnin', be a
house burnin' and a nigger fryin'. Somebody laughed loudly.

The night settled. People drifted off home. There was a chill in the air. March. Almost April. Spring comin' on. Eyes behind closed windows watched for firelike deer in the forest. The Black neighborhoods were very dark.

"I mean to do it, Florice," he said and his eyes were proof of his stubbornness. It was after a meeting of the women's auxiliary and she had lingered behind a little just to be with him a few more minutes. "But, Robert, they'll get you. A colored man got to say only so much if he wants to live. You know that."

She knew there was no use talking to him now. There was a stubborn will in him that was part of his strength and part of what made him wonderful to her. In a few years, his will would bring her very close to death, but that was one thing she was not given to know ahead of time. "I mean to do it. I got to go back to the pulpit this Sunday and I got to hold up my head. This is my work. I mean to preach the word; not some weak-kneed washed-out version of the Gospel." He had not told the congregation to wait patiently for the Lord, he had not quieted things down, and Joe Gray had died anyway, so what difference would it make now? He had to live day by day with the knowledge that he had sent Joe away with no real answer, and, by God, he would make it up or he'd leave the church.

"Miss Rebecca," he said, his eyes turned on her with all his love showing, "you do your work and you think folks don't see you special, but folks talk. They know you saved the Lowe's baby only they just don't know how. God calls us to different vineyards, and I do believe I've found out who I really am."

The NAACP was invited to meet at the church. By the end of a year Robert was president, and those who didn't like it either dropped off coming to church or changed their minds. Florice got used to a certain amount of worry, knowing that Robert had made himself and Joe Gray a symbol in the town. Though eventually the Joe Gray case sunk into the memories of even the Klan, the work quietly continued—a steady, even pushing at the evil which never went away and which Robert devoutly worked against. People began to come to him when they had some trouble with white folks. Sundays rolled around and around and more and more sermons were about the hatred they had to fight and the courage it took to ''stand up for Jesus,'' and then Florice began to love him more for his courage than for his charm, and that was her undoing.

1936

Mount Olive AME Church was not yet to know the delight of shared scandal, at least if it depended on Rebecca and Robert. Their love for each other and their out-and-out lust was, in public, as controlled as English tea, and as private. They were both frightened of their passion. Having experienced before the destruction caused by truth, they shut down as much as they could; unwilling to step into the bloody arena again. What they couldn't shut down seeped out as the truth will, in glances, in the scent he wore to services, in the way she used her hands. The knowledge that when she turned smartly and sashayed down the church hall, he would just barely be able to hide his excitement was delicious to Florice, had kept her going during long nights when she bit her teeth, so wanting she was.

The Rev. Robert Brown was not the same ethereal intellectual Theodore had been, but he had a roots wisdom that scoured the earth for answers. She loved him because he could bore through the lie and find the scare underneath. Together there was a Blackness about their love that called up African villages for her, and the primal river that ran through her veins had its rhythm altered by his touch. What was this man that he could recall the drums that were taken away by slavery simply by putting his lips on her wrist? One night, alone, she took her box out and touched each object, seeking some solid ground: the stone, the wool, the moss, the shell, and especially the sand dollar. But where was her wisdom? Sometime, she thought, sometime I do feel like a motherless chile, a *long* way from home; so far away that I won't never get home. So far away that it felt like God had left her behind, and He was laughin at her havin' to face this temptation twice. What was He tellin' her? What was she tellin' herself? Rebecca, Rebecca, Robert had said, what can there ever be for us? She had answered, we've got to have it all, and thought to herself, Oh, God, I can't, I can't dig no well with a teaspoon no second time.

For six years they had lived in and around their passion. Rebecca, the Ladies Auxiliary president, Rebecca, the Star of Bethlehem Circle secretary, Rebecca burned in her black dress and thought of that story she had long ago heard Theodore talk about—of Lancelot and his love, and how she was saved from the fire only to be cut off from her own fire, forever.

They went to the circus one day, she and Robert with the youth group. She wore her yellow daisy dress. It was soft, much softer than the dark blue church outfit. It was Robert's favorite. The day's sunlight had crept in slowly and this early afternoon it splashed on the daisy dress a little timidly. Florice thought of adjusting her stockings just as Robert walked up. "Mighty pretty we're lookin' today in our yellow, like a pure meadow on a July noon." His voice made her paper tremble. She was holding the list of children they were taking to the afternoon show. They would have to sit in the colored section away from the good seats and behind the tent's post, but that wasn't cooling down the excitement of the twenty youngsters crowding around the bus's door. The bus from George Washington Carver High School had been lent by Dr. Bishop, whose pompousness stuck like glue to his upper tongue. He oiled up to the gathering "to see that the bus didn't give them any trouble starting." Robert was cordial, and Florice spoke, though she thought she'd rather be in debt to a rattlesnake. "Just the two of you goin', eh?" He was definitely sniffin' around, thought Florice; she should have worn the navy blue outfit. "My missus's feelin' a little under the weather," Robert explained. He was very casual; Florice got busy lining up children to board the bus. She was trapped in her daisy dress.

They had looked at each animal act, one after the other. She saw Robert that day at the circus with her children, and got lost in a domestic fantasy, floating back and forth between the lion behind the bars and the lion behind the daisies. Something she remembered about a western wind and small rain from the Catholic school back home. "Oh that my love were in my arms," she thought, " 'cause I got a storm by the tail."

Robert, whose looks were that of the African warrior she knew in dreams, had gently brushed her collar. "Miss Florice? You better wake up there and check these animals out! That has got to be the most beautiful cat in captivity, except yours truly, of course."

"Now Reverend, you know what the Bible says about pride," she teased. As he flashed his startling smile, she felt the chills down her back, not for passion this time, but for fear. They were both "in captivity"; they were both caged. And you got to be free, she thought, to get to the promised land. You surely got to be free.

1937

The adult Sunday school was into its last five minutes. The subject for the day had been the miracles of Jesus. Robert usually taught that class, though sometimes he had a substitute and often he was late because of more pressing duties. Today he had been there for the entire class. "Well, I guess we're almost through for today," he said, gathering up his papers.

"Rev," a voice from the back row asked, "time for a question?"

"Certainly, Mr. Brooks."

Florice had turned in her seat to see who had spoken. She never missed a class if she could help it. Seeing Robert teach was a thrill for her. It was a way to be in his company, feel his spirit, and watch his mind work and she loved every minute of it.

Mr. Brooks spoke slowly. "Well Rev, I was wondering if you thought miracles still happen today?"

Robert was never frivolous or careless with his church members, no matter how silly he might think the question was, and he didn't think this was a silly question. "Mr. Brooks, when a baby gets born perfectly, or one of my church members really accepts Jesus, or a Black man truly gets justice in the courts then I know God works in the world and yes, I think miracles still happen."

Mr. Brooks leaned back in his chair. "Yes," he said, "I know Rev, but that's different. Like in the Bible, Jesus used his hands, you know, to heal people. He raised Lazarus from the dead. Do it happen like that anymore?"

Robert looked a little like he wished that question hadn't

been asked. He was sorry he had used the example of a baby being born. Mr. Brooks had a son who was blind. He was aware of Florice staring at her watch, and pulled his eyes away from her deliberately. "Some say so, Mr. Brooks, some say so. Now I don't know about bringing people back here who have gone on, but some say healing hands do exist." He looked at the short fat man who wanted a clear straightforward answer. "I believe," Robert hesitated, "I believe there are those among us on earth who have the gift."

The class of fifteen people stopped gathering their things to leave and everyone sat still. "I do believe there are those who have healing hands, and somehow the Lord works through them. It's not them, you see, it's still the Lord. His spirit is there using those hands for his work. And that is what I believe."

Mrs. Willacy spoke up, a church founder. "That's the devil's work." Her voice was hard and obviously hostile.

Then she remembered she was speaking to her pastor. "With respect, Rev, I just do believe we don't have no business puttin' ourselves up there with the Master. And folks ain't got no business usin' these roots and things. It's the devil's work." She looked directly at Florice. No one in the room could have missed it. "Some folks get to thinkin' they bettern' other folks. Sometimes folks who has these gifts thinks they too good for other folks, and then that's when you can tell it's not from God a'tall, it's from the devil." Florice turned her head slightly and stared at Dorothy Willacy. She had heard stories, they had all heard stories, that was all. They had no real information. Bits and pieces here and there. Still her heart was going a little faster. What would Robert say now? She must keep her composure. She must not let them see her get nervous. Had someone she trusted exposed her? The class time was up but nobody looked anxious to go put the flowers on the altar or get ready for the service. Robert cleared his throat. "Well, you know, Sister Willacy," he said, patiently, "St. Paul tells us God gives us all gifts of the spirit. I believe you will find in First Corinthians where he says some of us have the gift of healing given by the Spirit, and to some of us is even given the gift of working miracles. And some of us have the gift of speech. Perhaps that is your gift, Sister Willacy.'' He was smiling warmly at the old woman.

Sister Willacy put her handkerchief neatly into her bag. She was trying very hard to keep her place of authority as church mother. She thought, Perhaps he is right. She had spoken well at the women's meeting last night. At least three of the women had said she should have been a preacher. She managed a small smile.

''And you know,'' Robert was saying to the whole class, ''we must develop our gifts so that we can use them to the glory of God.'' He stopped talking and looked intently at nothing as if remembering. ''St. Paul says we must love one another also, no matter what our gifts . . . yes . . . yes that's in the same passage,'' and here he looked at Dorothy Willacy very intently, ''because we are all members of the body of Christ. Well ladies and gentlemen, we must go; we'll all be late for service.'' Florice smiled very slightly in Dorothy Willacy's direction and said good morning. She spoke to a few other people, and made her way toward the service. She did so love that man. There was just a little bounce in her step, not so you'd notice if you didn't know her.

Dorothy Willacy was still thinking about her gift. Somewhere inside herself she knew she had just been reprimanded, but she couldn't quite figure out how. Then just as she was ready to leave the room, the president of the Star of Bethlehem Circle asked her to be the speaker for the next meeting and on her way to the sanctuary she was concentrating only on a possible topic for that occasion.

* * *

After love-making; in her kitchen. Jessie and the children were visiting her parents in Charlotte, an unexpected and delightful surprise for them. Robert sat pensively at the kitchen table. ''But how did she come to be so suspicious, I wonder?''

Florice was warming a cup of soup for him, her back to him at the stove. She was wearing a casual wraparound

dress, pink with flowers."I don't know, Robert, I just don't
know. It leaks out, I guess. There've been a few people here
and there through the years that I've helped. Never did go
out of my way to let people know. Never really did want
folks to know. I didn't ask for this healin' gift, darlin'." She
turned around and looked at him. "I just got it. One day I
knew I could do it. It was like God asked me to do it. Scared
me to death, I'll tell you."

Robert laughed and motioned for her to come sit on his
lap. Florice giggled. "No Robert, you've got to go. You been
here a long time. Folks'll be missing you!"

"Come on, Miss Lady, over here right now. Sit. Precious
little time we have like today. Precious little time we'll ever
have like this!" She pulled down all the shades and felt the
love flow over and around her. She would never be happier
than at this moment.

"You know, you could decide to really go after it." He
looked into her brown eyes, so close to his.

"What do you mean?" she asked.

"You could decide to take God up on His offer. Be public
about it. You wouldn't be the first lady ever done it."

"Oh no, oh no, I *couldn't*." She hid her face in his shoulder in horror. "How could I live? I wouldn't be me. I'd be a
freak, and people like that Mrs. Willacy, they'd have me
tarred and feathered and run out of town or something just
as bad. It's too horrible to think about. Those good Christian
people, they'd be just like Mac was, only worse." She shuddered.

"Well, I just wondered," he said thoughtfully, rubbing
her arm. "I just wondered if you ever thought about leaving
the womb." She looked at him quizzically. "You know," he
said,"the womb of safety."

"How about you?" Florice got down from his lap and
pulled a chair up close to him at the table. "How about you?
You know I've never asked you to leave her." He looked
very serious. Suddenly the young lover look he had worn just
a few seconds before had turned to the look of an older man,
sober, slightly stern.

"Florice," he said, "I just will not do that." He put his

left hand over hers on the table. The wedding band was obtrusive. He didn't want to hurt her. That was something he had never wanted to do. Her eyes watered. He put his hand in his lap. She got up quickly, busying herself with something at the kitchen counter.

"You asked me about leaving the womb," she said, "I just thought I'd return the favor."

"It's not the same thing," he was quick to answer. "It's not safety, it's principal! I'm married. I took vows. I'm a man of the cloth. I took vows!"

"But, my love, you aren't living them." She was sure of herself now. "That's not right either. We could both be free then, Robert. You and I could live the truth for ourselves. We could both fly then, instead of being tied down to this fear." They saw in each other's eyes for once that rare gift of nakedness that we so seldom give one another. There it was, the truth, riding between them on the light between her eyes and his. She would not look away. "We could both be ourselves. With you maybe I would have the courage to be all of who I am and maybe if we were together, maybe you could truly bind up the brokenhearted and God's promise in us could really be fulfilled." He shifted his gaze and it broke the truth into a thousand splinters, but he had heard it and she knew he had heard it.

"I have to go," he said, "I'll be late."

To protect themselves, some species mimic other life forms through the use of color and form. Other moths have no defense, but protect themselves by imitating those who do.

1938

The speech at the fish fry rose and fell like white caps in the ocean. The tingling music of southern softness, the drawn out second syllable of laughter fell on the black cushion of female presence, rich in browns and punctuated with fertile smiles.

The college girl, conspicuous in her felt cloche and brown wool jacket, seemed a modern interruption to time in the Black Southland. She had a nervousness that she hoped only showed in her dangling earrings which trembled a bit too much. When Harriet drove up to the campus in her father's old Chevy truck, she was on the edge of serious trouble.

Alice was the chief cook at this affair. No one challenged her absolute command over fish frying. No one who had ever heard of the sea islands would have had the nerve to do so. She stood over a large black iron pot, poking, turning, knowing just exactly what to do, and enjoying the knowing. There was a wood fire under the pot, and it was very hot work. Alice kept wiping her forehead with her sleeve. This was the opening picnic for new students.

Harriet's father looked confused and a little embarrassed. "Y'all know where 'fessor Benedict is?" Some of the girls came around to help him manage with directions and bags, and Harriet got out of the car. She began to have trouble keeping back the tears. "Papa, I'll see you Thanksgiving, OK?" She looked a little older than most of the girls. They ushered her into the girls' dormitory and the raggedy Chevy truck pulled off, carrying with it her home and safety.

Alice mentioned Harriet to Florice that night after the picnic. She was drowsy and worn out and said she "never wanted to see no fish again in life."

"And did you see the new girl?" asked Florice.

"Oh, yeh, gurl, I see her. She nice lookin' but kinda sad, maybe just leavin' home, you know."

At breakfast the next day, Alice said, "There she go."

"Who, Alice?" Florice had not yet had her second cup of coffee.

"The new gurl, Florice."

Harriet was sitting over a cup of coffee looking like she wanted to jump into it and sink to the bottom.

The new students got duty work first. Harriet was a hard worker, but always teary. One day sitting at the table she ran out of the dining hall and didn't show up for dinner or duty that night at all. The next day Florice took Harriet's apron down from its peg and took it over to Harriet who was staring at the green beans. "Here, honey, you forgot this." Harriet turned around and met the eyes of a mother who was not a mother. She sighed. "Thanks, Miss Florice."

Florice decided to get right to the point. "Honey, you want company? I got a evening with nothing to do but plan what y'all gonna eat next week and I already know that." Harriet smiled and nodded. "Yes ma'am," she whispered.

"Well anybody can spot a young woman in trouble," she answered the silence. Alice kept washing the pots.

With only a farming father for a family, she had decided that coming to school was better than disgracing her father. And where would she go when the school turned her out? She rocked and cried and rocked and cried and used up all Miss Florice's clean handkerchiefs. And, oh God, he had already paid her tuition, and oh, God, what would the deacons say back home, and "Oh Lord, Miss Florice what am I gonna do?

Florice soothed the mind with presence of Spirit, and the body with innumerable cups of herbal tea. She provided a warm shoulder and a cool head. The herbs were now in the backyard of the rooming house and everyone who lived there felt welcomed by the sight of Miss Florice's herbal garden, as it came to be known.

Actually Rebecca Florice did not know what Harriet was "gonna do" but she believed in holding on. And sometimes she thought holding on was all there was to faith.

"Let me think on this, Harriet. Got to be a way to keep body and soul from fallin' apart. You ain't the first young woman made a mistake, and God knows you ain't gonna be the last. And where's your young man?"

"He wants to marry me, but there isn't any money and he wants schoolin' too, and I just messed it all up!" She dissolved again.

"Well, Lord, we ain't got no problem then. Ronald Johnstone will just have to back up on them plans. Don't you worry about a thing for another minute."

"But, Miss Florice, he's in the Army!" She blew her nose, and looked out the window. Finally, just before curfew, Harriet walked back to the dormitory in the blowing rain. She was tight and feeling sick and there was no sidewalk and no road and no way. Only mud that sucked at your feet.

Alice came home to find Florice gone to bed, or at least her light was out very early. She lifted her hand to knock, and changed her mind. In her room, Florice was deep into her mirror self, looking into a dark pool for reflections of truth.

Saturday morning it was still raining. The fall had come finally, and on her way to the corner grocery store, Florice watched the play of leaves on leaves. They went in and out of each other, pushing, dancing, being pulled this way and that. Dead leaves still hanging on to the tree, but still dead. The branches of fir trees bounced up and down in rhythm. She reached into her coat pocket and found a packet of herbs, forked larkspur. Oh yes, she remembered, she had thought of taking that to Selma. A model T Ford drove by. Making a racket, she thought. Tomorrow was Sunday again. They did seem to come around fast. And there was a Woman's Auxiliary meeting she was in charge of tonight. She saw one of the college girls come into her view from the opposite direction, running. But running with panic. She couldn't catch her breath at first. She held her side in pain.

"Oh, Miss Florice, come quick please! Harriet done took something, and she's bleedin', she bleedin'!"

There was no time to think, only get there, only get there. She was forty-five, and she wouldn't remember until that night when her calves started aching that she had run all the way from Washington Street to the dormitory and up a flight of stairs. Her mind said forked larkspur, forked larkspur, get her legs up and make her drink forked larkspur.

The floor was silent except for one girl weeping in a corner, terrified. Florice had no trouble knowing which room. They were all standing in the hall, starkly confronted with the common terror of being female.

Harriet was drooping over a wastebasket, vomiting up whatever she had taken, and dressed only in a bloody slip, the curves of her vulnerability outlined in red. Florice rapped out orders. "Get me some hot water, and a teapot, or something to pour it from," she said sharply. "Get me some towels." She moved to pick Harriet up. Two of the girls helped get her on the bed and got blood on their skirts and hands. "Three pillows and three blankets," said Florice. They were handed to her from somewhere. The pillows went under the feet. The blankets went on top. Harriet shuddered. Somewhere down the hall, somebody was having hysterics. She brewed the herbs and poured them down Harriet, who choked on the taste and tried to push the cup away. Florice grabbed her shoulders. She was still bleeding. The towels between her legs were turning bright red. She forced some more of the liquid down Harriet by holding her jaw open. "Girl, don't you want this baby to have a chance of comin' here? What you mean, tryin' to turn a river?" Harriet, close to passing out, felt the strength in the hands on her shoulders, and then she had to clutch her belly and the pain made her cry out. Florice pushed Harriet's hands away, and laid her own hands on the young womb. A rush of hope left her fingers and palms. In a few minutes Florice changed the towels, and as the bleeding stopped, Harriet relaxed into exhausted sleep.

Her eyes were wide, and out of focus, and her legs shook. She sat there like that for a long time, watching carefully as the young woman slept. I did it, she thought. Theodore, I did do it.

Alice's little tea table was comforting and her chatter was so good that they had sat up much later than either one had planned. She should go to church tomorrow, but Lordy, it sure would be good to sleep instead. In a few more minutes she said goodnight and went into her own room. Harriet would need care, she thought, and Dr. Benedict would have to be told. She went to sleep wishing she had a house of her own.

When the adult is fully formed and conditions are right, it bursts the pupal shell and crawls out.

1938

Dr. Benedict was a sturdy man. That may have been the most outstanding thing about him. He wanted to make this place a college Black folks could be proud of, that his children would be proud of. And he was doing it out of sheer will, even as he was unaware that his will sometimes ran head-on into his objectives. It was that Monday morning that he asked to see her. She knew he had probably heard what happened Saturday afternoon. She straightened her stocking seams and pulled at her skirt. It wouldn't do to go in there looking slovenly. Or with an attitude; she thought carefully. There were other jobs as cooks, maybe.

The secretary sent her in. Florice was taller than Dr. Benedict. He drew himself up to his entire height and cleared his throat. "Good morning, Miss Letenielle. And how are you this beautiful day?" Too nervous to be encouraged by his tone, Florice answered quietly, "Fine, sir, and yourself?"

"We just couldn't be better; couldn't be better." She thought she had seen him act "nice-nasty" before. Maybe he didn't know. But what could he want, then?

"Miss Letenielle, how are things over in the dining hall?" She was opening her mouth just as he continued. "Y'all just let us know because we want our girls to be happy, you know, and healthy."

Oh Lord, she thought. "Healthy." She imagined he was going to launch into his usual chapel speech about mental, physical and spiritual strength and purity. But instead he said, "Aren't you living in the Rose Tree Rooming House for single ladies?" Florice was conscious of being too hot in her coat, and she hoped her hair was still in place. She could feel a few strands hanging down by her ear. She answered quietly.

"What would you think of moving closer to us and living in a house? Do you think you'd like that? I guess you're wondering why I'm asking you these questions," he said, not giving her any time to answer. He laughed to himself. "Well, there's a house across the street there, a two-story white house at the far corner of the campus and that house is owned by Bluford Street Methodist church. They are feeling they'd like to make that house available to the college as a gift. And I won't go into the details, but we'd like you to live in it and take care of it, you know. Keep up the place and make it nice for campus guests and maybe have the girls over from time to time. It would be your home, you understand, but we'll help you with the expenses in exchange for this service. Maybe you could teach them a little about how to manage a home. Women still need to know that, you know." Agreeing with himself, he smiled. Florice said simply, "Yes sir, I'd like that." Should she ask him here and now? Her mind was racing, but she wasn't apprehensive anymore. This was it. She smiled her most dazzling smile and plunged in. "What would you say to my keeping girls in the house who need a little mothering, sir? You know our girls are sometimes real young at heart. They get a little lost and homesick. Would a few days with me be all right, sir? Of course, I could see to the regulations, you understand." There was a brief silence. He adjusted his pipe, which was carefully placed in an ashtray on the desk.

"And just what are we going to do about Harriet, Miss Lentenielle?" She was careful not to show any emotion. He was not a man you could trap. "Well, I know she can't stay in school now, but . . ."

"I'll give you two weeks to find her a place. Two weeks in the house, you see. After that . . . this kind of thing," he shook his head, "looks bad with the board. Church people. Come back in two weeks." Suddenly he seemed very preoccupied. "Well, then, here are the keys to the house. You can move in any time. Anything you need, call my secretary." He shook her hand firmly. Didn't do to get too involved with these things. Just keep it safe. Still, he thought, she was not an ordinary woman. He liked her; in spite of himself.

Finally when she reached the kitchen, she let it out: "God still handin' out blessin's in the kingdom!" she said, aloud and to herself. He hadn't expelled her immediately, that was the miracle. And two weeks was long enough to put that child's life back together somehow and, oh God, she hoped the girls wouldn't start any gossip about a healing or any "powers" she had. That would be all Dr. Benedict would need to hear.

Alice was disgruntled. "Umph. Wonder who told him?" she said. "Some folks got to always be messin' in other folks' business." Florice looked at Alice, realizing for the first time that she would be moving out of the boardinghouse where they had lived together for over ten years. She put her hand on Alice's shoulder.

"It's only right down the street, girl." Alice turned quickly.

"Time to put out the lunch," she said, under her breath.

1939

November. Their legs wrapped around this impossibility.
"Why did you have to give it a name?" she said in desperate
fever. "Why did you have to open that awful door?" "We
opened it together, baby. I ain't done nothin' all by myself."
He was pained, but not so you could hold on to the pain. He
had always told the truth; he had never said he would leave
home. She had to admit that. What he touched in her was
her own truth and that is like licking ice in the Delta sun.
She just didn't have the strength to give that up.

"Why you talkin' bout this, Florice? You know I love you.
I cannot leave home. I never said I could leave home."

"Robert, what am I gonna do? You got me turnin' every
which way with this, with us. Don't you see what we've gone
and done?"

"I got to go, honey, I really got to go. Ain't nothin' I can
do. You and me, we just not meant to be married. I'm a
minister! Can't you see that? I got to go." He undid his body
from hers, and rubbed her back slowly as he raised himself
up from the bed. "God knows you sweet; Lord, you a sweet
woman." There was a deep sadness in his eyes that he usually was very careful to hide.

It was always her bed, her house. There was never any-
place else to go, and there was never enough time to feel it
good; they had to be so careful, and besides, she always
ended up feeling like she'd lost him before she knew she
would. Like he was already gone. She'd be missin' him while
he was comin' inside her, and while she was slidin' up that
mountain, she was always sliding down at the same time.
But it was a glorious snowfallin' beauty. She always wanted

the flakes to make some sound when they fell, 'cause if they did, maybe it would all be real; and then, when the fallin' was over he'd be gone, and so would the snow; and so would the snow. It was ripplin' pretty, Lord, it was pretty, it was the mighty clouds of joy, but it was knowin that she would never never hear the sound of that snow that tore at her with every time. Still, she couldn't end it. It would end of its own accord, or it wouldn't end. She couldn't and he couldn't or he wouldn't. She wasn't sure which.

Robert *was* his body. A man whose sort would have walked the streets gladly offering himself to every pretty woman he met, but his itch for respectability and his guilt had kept him afraid of knowing his own lush garden. In Florice he had found a woman who could show him his garden, and whose own sense of respectability would keep it a secret. Her depth met his at a place where neither of them had ever been. He was frightened of his love for her; it was too much, and his life had been built on never showing how far his feelings went. He had built a fine, middle class Black church where there were *two* choirs, one that sang gospel, and one that sang "arranged" spirituals, to satisfy those who were a little more "discriminating." He had found himself a wife who loved being a minister's wife and who loved him decently. And now he had himself a woman who, though terrified of tomorrow, wasn't afraid to answer her deepest needs today, and who loved him, not decently, but with extremities he had only known in himself.

She had helped him open a door to himself marked courage, and that only deepened his love for her. Now, he knew what it really meant to be on the line. Now, he could step over to freedom. He could reach out his hand to it, and carry it home, if he could find home. Liberty, and the "yoke of bondage." What kind of hell was this freedom anyway? And where was his peace? He had never wanted to know this much about himself. There were too many limits. She knew better than to ask. She knew better at the time she did it. But she had crossed over. The bridge had crashed behind her, and though she knew he would not pick his way through the rocks to get to her there was only one road left to travel so she took it, seeing nothing ahead but a landscape familiar in its terrible loneliness.

"Now look, girl. I love you more than I'm due to. More than I should. You know that." He was weary, not of her, but of knowing limits. He had known limits all his life. Fences, pockets, barriers. Do not enter. Colored waiting room. White only. Thou shalt not. commit. anything. Her fire was glowing. The gray coals made little clicking noises. The clock ticked regularly. 3:30 P.M. Robert ran his fingers around his tight white collar and squirmed slightly in the straight chair. Florice sat a respectable distance across the room, looking at the empty coffee cups. He could have been any pastor visiting any well-thought-of single lady, president of the Ladies' Auxiliary and secretary of the Star of Bethlehem. "My baby," he said, "my sweet sugar, what'd you think we *could* do about this?"

"Ain't no sense in livin' the way we do and sinnin' for it, and not doin' something about it!" she breathed. The windows rattled slightly with the November wind. All the girls had left for Thanksgiving break. The street was very quiet. She was now almost forty-six and he was forty-five. Old enough to know better. Too old for such foolishness, they would have said. They would have *all* said. But no one was going to have the pleasure of squeezing her between their teeth. Though she would have given up such consolation for love, they didn't know that. They would never know that.

November in North Carolina. When there isn't any fall left, and there isn't any winter worth its salt. November. Just what it is. Robert had left his chair and was standing in front of the drawn curtains as if for a portrait. He opened his arms, and she walked into them.

1940

It was Saturday night. She had been washing the dishes in Ivory and he came to the back door to say goodbye. Now there were cups, saucers, recklessly thrown, unrinsed, into the drainer. Robert had just left, having weakly apologized that his church was calling him to Pittsburgh, and that he couldn't say no, and that his wife was after all his wife, and that the move would be good for her, and she knew . . . she knew he had asked to be transferred, and she knew that no-body would be changing churches at his age except to be-come a bishop, and . . . she knew it couldn't go on forever now, didn't she?

"Florice, least you could say is goodbye." Florice was not a door slammer; she was not a slammer or a screamer. All her life she had believed that there were certain things you didn't let other people see you doing. Having a crying fit was one. Losing your nerve was one. Her face was hard, and her mouth was hers and hers only and not his anymore when he said, "Please." When Robert had backed out the door, Florice slammed it shut, and screamed. In the morning there were two broken plates, several clean saucers in the sink, and a floor streaked with dried tears and Ivory Snow.

"And, girl, didn't you know that was Rev Brown's last service? How come you didn't come, girl?" Alice stared straight ahead using up all her patience with Selma.

"Go on, Selma, what's the story?"

"You ain't never seen such a disgrace and to-do, confessin' in church, and all about that baby, well, I never, Alice." Selma's mop was going as fast as her mouth. She had become very conscious of her "place in the community" as she called it, since having been hired at Centenary College, and was now very moral when the occasion suited. Mrs. Benedict had not succeeded in getting her hair tied down, but Selma had picked up the habit of cleaning in her hat on days when her hair was truly in an outrageous condition. The worn satin flower bobbed up and down on her brim as she passed on this delicious gossip to Alice, who had her own quiet opinion of Reverend Brown, and had refused to attend the farewell service. She and Florice had simply respected each other's silence on this matter. Alice had welcomed his departure with relief, only because she was tired of waiting for the inevitable pain it would cause her friend. Selma mopped and bobbed. Her hat was desperately hanging on to the side of her head. "Well," she said only after an appropriate dramatic pause, "Addie Mae stood up yesterday morning with confession on her mind. It was weighin' heavy on her mind. And you know, Alice, you could just tell Addie Mae took her sweet time startin' that confession, cause she wore her green hat with the pink rose in it and her green suit, and her white gloves with the one button at the wrist and, oh honey, she was struttin' her stuff! And Rev Brown he said last Sunday 'fore you comes to the Lord's Supper you got to have a clean heart. Well, God knows there's many a nigger done come to the Lord's table with a heart that needs to be washed and hung out to dry! And Addie's all the time goin by Florice's house worryin' that good woman to death 'bout how she needs to unburden her heart to someone, and now she got to confess in public in everybody's face!

"Rev Brown, he got through the sermon fine and he was callin' folks to the altar and saying those who wanted to testify should 'come forth' and Addie Mae straightened her dress real good, and made like she was just a little shy, you know, 'course everybody know she ain't never been shy; she didn't get no baby bein' shy . . . and just as the choir got to 'Oh Lamb of God, I come,' she stood up. Rev Brown, he turned and motioned the choir to hum. He said 'Addie, you got somethin' to tell us this mornin'?' Addie Mae said, 'Rev, I got to tell how my heart been hurtin' me. Just painin' my breast, and the Lord told me to go see the good sister Florice.

And the Lord said, "Addie Mae go see Sister Florice, for she got a good heart" and so I did. And sister Florice she told me to forgive this man who did unto me, Rev Brown, and to confess and say I's sorry and that I would be forgiven. And so I am here this mornin', Rev, to say that I have sinned greatly and I am truly sorry, Rev, even though that Donel, he done sinned too, and he done treated me bad, Rev, and left me with no money and with this here youngun, but I'm real sorry, Rev, and I won't never do nothing that bad again and also, Rev, I forgive Donel with all my heart and I hope he's happy even if he won't marry me, and this his baby." And Addie Mae sat down.

"And the Rev, he looked sort of confused, you know, and tried to catch Miss Florice's eye only she was staring straight ahead at the altar flowers like they had withered in front of her eyes, and she never did look at the Rev at all when he said, 'Praise the Lord for his works and for Miss Florice who works through the Lord, and let us all thank the Lord for Addie's testimony this morning and welcome her to the Lord's table,' and the choir started up loud again singin', 'Just as I am.' " Selma took a breath. Alice shook her head and said nothing, hoping that Selma would decide she was struck speechless with her story.

"Well, lemme go mop some more floors. Lord, them girls do make a mess!" Alice knew Selma would try the story out on someone else now, someone who would be sufficiently impressed with her opening come-on: "Girl, I got somethin' to tell you!"

That he could leave her, that he could just do that like the leaves fall from the trees and let a naked skeleton stand; like the sun could leave a darkened cover for our bare heads; that he could leave her exposed in a rasping desert of grainy air and not look back—where was the logic in that if not the love? Where did it make sense? She had hoped something would happen to him—to her—something to put off the inevitable end of the fantasy that she would one day be his. He had been the reasonable one. She had always counted on being grounded by him. She of the rainbow lights, she of the mysterious lore and herbs that made others whole. Many thought of Florice as practical and down-to-earth even though she was a little "strange," but she knew of struggles between bread and incense that few experience. Though she had balanced others, Robert had been her balance, her safe port in a sea of smoky faith and wild fanciful vision, her touchstone of the mundane, where she could come to rest from her own wanderings. He was so present, so grounded in his reality.

He continued to come back to her—in dreams, in smells, in visions too sensual to be of the past. And the knowledge that it would forever be the past became ever-present, like a toothache. Cowardly, cowardly pain, she thought; not to be able to kill him in herself with deed or dream. There were days between these memories that were full of loving and caring, but she was not free. She looked at the world through a transparent veil. Times she could pull the veil aside were glorious with color, but something would tug at it always, would sneak back in and suck at her joy like an evil child. It fed on her through all the long months of that year.

Many larvae add twigs and leaves, bits of grass outside of the cocoon, and build the walls in a double or triple layer. Through the long winter months the cocoon hangs from the twig like a dead leaf.

1940–Winter

It looked like there were no more doors gonna open for her and no more ways to turn it round. He had brought her to the shining light of love returned. For the only time in her life, he had brought her to that secret spot, that place where her soul was balanced and the angels hummed, and now that she had lost it, all she had left was the desire not to feel. What did she do to end up with nothin'? What had she ever done but answer the call? She carried her anger like a sack of fire, and it burned with a toxic fury that left her exhausted and drained after each dream.

Lean and dark, a young black leopard was chasing her, running her down, pinning her to the ground and taking her with his sleek body. Taking her to the summit of her pleasure, and then she would wake up suddenly and be laid low by the desire, the grief and the shame. The desire for him, the grief that she had it still, and the shame that she had been truly touched by him again; that she loved it, and that she would still do almost anything to have him back.

Her smile was strange these days. Had she seen herself in the mirror she might have been warned by the fever-splayed eyes shot through with fire. She often found her mind wandering around in New Orleans. She remembered the Dambella, the great source of life and then she decided. She'd remember enough. She'd remember enough or she would be damned. Probably both, she thought, smiling with her mouth. There was less and less of Florice living behind her eyes. She remembered the Petro loa who were wicked and terrible and trafficked in sacrifices. So. Finally.

A Friday winter afternoon. Florice locked herself in. She

would be theirs for ten days. Carefully, just so. There would be no mistake. The gods would know exactly who it was. She worked late. Without eating, without needing to use the bathroom. This was something she could do about it. Something she could say. Without saying it, without standing on a street corner, throwing her head back and wailing that somehow, somehow it wasn't meant to be this way and there had been a mistake. Her mouth was slightly open. She had left herself. Slipping into a dark corner. Slipping on a thread. Getting thinner and thinner and disappearing into a howl. But for now she saw only this, only that she must do something about this pain. And someone would find it, and her, and someone would finally know that it wasn't fair that she had suffered and she could scream in relief, finally, silently, and forever. She was looking for her scissors. She began to turn out kitchen drawers, frantic with the decision to finish this thing. She took her long hair down from its wound braids. It fell onto her shoulders. Heavy. Black. One long lock. Cut off and wound around in her favorite style.

The house was very cold in the December night, but there were no chill bumps on her arms and she left the back door open and went out without her coat. Wind blew in and ruffled some scraps of blue cotton on the kitchen table, pieces of rope and a few strands of hair. Anyone passing would have heard someone nailing briefly and then silence. The screen was banging against the house and she pulled it closed quickly just as the winter light broke into morning.

Saturday

The pain was welcome. At least you could blame your agony on it and not say to anybody that you wanted to die because your sanctuary from the storm, your warming place, your seed fire had left you and you would never be all the way alive again. You could hold on to the pain and not call it hatred. You could say you were sick and maybe you had the flu. She dragged to work and dragged home, and wondered how long it would be before she had to give in and lie down and let them take her.

Sunday

Had been a hard day. There was church. And then all that to-do afterwards about choir practice and who would sing the solo. Rochetta Gilbert had followed her to the ladies' room and stood in there doing something to her hair while Florice closed herself off and tried to vomit.

Monday

In the bustle of Christmas excitement on campus, they didn't notice her frequent swallows, and how many times she had excused herself from the dining room. Alice was very busy with the Christmas week menus and by the end of the day, her own head was splitting. Another nail in. There was a big rat out there near the trash can this morning. She must get Mr. Newell at the school to see to some poison.

Tuesday

Got to work early. Nobody witnessed the fall, up the steps to the Kirkfield union. She was still able to do most of her work, but the smell of food was getting harder and harder to bear. That afternoon she dropped the cake bowl and spilled batter all over the floor. Her arm suddenly lost all its strength and jerked forward. Alice concerned but patient.

Wednesday

The Robert dream came. She laughed aloud when the cramps started. Like it was her period, they ran from her side down her leg. Alice wanted to know why she wore those ugly shoes to work, and were her feet painin' her. The walk home was slowly and carefully executed. She stopped once beside a large bush. Nothing would come up from her slightly bloated stomach.

Thursday

She went out to the tree that faced north at 3:00 A.M. First nail in the womb. She'd cause her own labor pains, she thought, and twisted her mouth. So she'd never have a baby; she'd have a doll. She'd have a doll. It would have his eyes, be his color. She started to laugh bitterly. Somebody would tell him she was a witch and he would feel right that he had left. The air was pre-dawn, chilling. She had to kneel suddenly with pain. The pain was running into her bones, the pain was running into her tears, turning her tears to ice.

Friday

Woke to vomit in her bed. Called in sick. There were only two more. Two more nails. Alice came by. Bless her. She had the flu. Alice knew that. Why did she come why did she always come. Put too much cover on her. Changed sheets. Washed.

Saturday

There was a reason. To put on a coat. There was a reason yesterday. Case someone saw her. Too hot all the time. Turn the heat down. Her hair was too dry. Gonna look like steel wire. Stand up. Her eyes rolled. Back and forth like a drunkard back and forth. Get fired drunk. The hammer was under the bed. Somewhere. There was only one nail left. Down. Down the stairs. Hold on tight. Open the damn door one more time and get cool at least. House was very dark. She wanted lights. Afraid. Must not sleep in the dark room. Not tonight.

Sunday

Ninth day. Wire it up and spit it out. Wire it up and spit it out. Why did she need to find it? Why wasn't it under the bed where she left it? Attic. Trunk. Only there has to be an end now. They said so back home. The old lady at the river who danced all night. No wire. No wire. Push these things over. So heavy these clothes. Under. Old Christmas decorations. Wire. Saliva on her chin. No dignity, Florice. No dignity left. He left you with no. Wire it up and spit it out. Under the stomach. Around the back. And tight. So long. It was too hot out here and under the place of pleasure until the blue was covered. It would be good. To dig. Be cool. Garden is mine. Die in it. Die there.

* * *

Alice knew this wasn't the flu. She was used to being patient and letting Florice talk at her own pace, but she had known for a long time that the thing with Robert Brown was dangerous. Because Florice had put it all there, everything Theodore had denied. Every feeling she ever had, all the love and all the selfishness. All the goodness and all the lust. All the joy for just bein' on the earth alive and all the fury at having joy denied. And somewhere, something had to give. And Alice knew in her very bones that Florice was going to have to pay for this one. She couldn't stand the silence any longer. They were going to have this one out, one way or another.

Florice was in the herb garden. It was, at the most, 40° outside. She stared straight ahead as if she heard nothing, and kept digging in her herbs around the section where the skull cap grew in the summer.

Alice spoke out of her dismay, gently. "An' what you out here diggin' for? Ain't nothin' gonna grow in this weather. Com'on gurl, we go into the house now. Up with you. Com'on gurl." There was only the sound of the passing cars. Florice was very silent. She would go into the pain and into the darkness and the end of it. Her stomach had been upset for so long that she was very thin. Alice noticed how much smaller her arms had become as she helped pull the nightgown down. She winced, noticing the bones outlined in Florice's back. "You get in bed for some rest and we have a nice mashed potato and you eat it for sure, right? That be good for your stomach and you eat it for sure, right? We got to feed you some.'' December evening was coming down at 5:30 in the afternoon and the windows rattled in the wind just a little. Alice turned on a light. ''We got to get some fight back in you, gurl.'' She mumbled to herself on the way downstairs. ''Lord, Lord what you gone and done gurl, what you gone and done?''

Florice opened her eyes briefly. They rested on a small china box Robert had given her in the flush of their affair. Then she closed her eyes again and the pain swept her past her memory.

Alice shivered, thinking about Florice's illness; knowing Florice as well as she did, she had her own ideas about the nature of this illness. Something was rotten somewhere, or she wasn't from ''de islands'', something unholy was sho goin' on heah, she thought. She could feel it. She could see it in the unnatural face of her friend. Love for Florice held her in the house, frightened as she was. Alice had always said she would never touch roots, never. She shook her head and peeled a potato, found some pipsissewa and made hot tea, hands shaking. And she was so good, too good to lose her soul over loving some man. Lord, Lord. She shook her head back and forth and began to pray under her breath as the potato boiled.

The garbage can was always in the backyard next to the big tree. It was a strange tree, full of knots and grew somehow mostly on one side, its branches reaching out toward the north rather than the south; the south side had a big gash in it where some children had ridden a branch off and Florice had worried about the tree, and doctored on it with black tar. Alice lifted the garbage can lid and slammed it closed. ''Sho is cold, for true,'' she mumbled to herself, and was about to go back into the house when her eye caught a blue scrap of something on the rounded corner of the tree. Alice frowned and took two tentative steps forward. ''Oh, my Lord, my Lord Jesus, have mercy on us all, his chillun,'' and she caught herself on the tree just before she fell forward all the way. Her hand landed on a doll, nailed firmly to the tree, and on Florice's hair which was blowing fiercely in the wind, on the doll's head. The doll's face was turned toward the tree. There were nine nails in it. Alice clawed at the ugly thing, desperately afraid, angry, and in agony for her dear love of a friend. All she knew at that moment was that she had to get those nails out, and as she tore at it, she began to repeat phrases she had known all her life. "The Lord is my shepherd," she began, "the Lord is my shepherd. Sweet Jesus, sweet Jesus, come by heah, come by heah." There was no mistaking it was Florice. An exaggerated copy. Cocoa colored. Long legged. Nine nails. One in the heart, two in the legs, and at least four in the abdomen and pelvic area; and a wire around the waist pulling it in so tight that the doll was almost all wire in the middle.

As she pulled at the doll, she heard a scream that tore at her own body, and the thing finally came off in her hands. Somehow, holding the image at arm's length, she found the kitchen. Florice was moaning upstairs. The floor creaked every time she'd toss violently in bed. Alice's hands shook so much she was having trouble untying and twisting the wire. She kept repeating "Lead us not into temptation, but deliver us from evil." It fell to the floor finally. "Deliver us from evil, but deliver us from evil," she had begun to stammer and then she smelled the burning potato and leaped to the stove to turn it off. Something would have to be done fast. If ah could just remember them spells, she thought, how to uncross evil, how to do it. She was climbing the stairs as fast as she could, but she had never been so weak and frightened, and her mind was racing, racing toward graveyard dust, and incenses, and she remembered the old ones putting a dime under somebody's tongue.

Florice was leaning over the wastebasket. She had tried for the toilet, but her legs were too weak now. She was sweating heavily, her gown as wet as if she had bathed in it. The pain had taken over her eyes completely and she was far away in her own hell. This is the time, Alice thought, it's now or we done lost her. She was standing at the bedroom door looking at the back of Florice's head. The doll's head flashed into Alice's mind. She brought her breath in sharply. The thick head of hair she was staring at that had been cut just enough to cover the head of a doll, was matted and had lost its luster. Alice smelled vomit and a musky odor she had never noticed about Florice. "What chu figur to do, just die? What chu believe, gurl, that the Lord promised you just what chu wanted?" Alice's voice was loud and angry. "That you come here for getting what chu want? What you think, the Lord gon keep you from trouble 'cause you Rebecca Florice? The Lord give you all them gifts for a reason. Not to be workin' wid no devils!" Alice's mouth tightened. Her teeth touched. She stayed in the doorway. Florice was almost on the floor, crouched, holding on to the bed. She rocked herself back and forth and made little pained noises. "If you gon die for true, you gon die and I can't save you. But if you gon die, you sho do talk some good talk, and that's it. What kind of talk you been talkin'? You been tellin' me to hold on, hold on, believe this, believe that. You sho do talk purty, Miss Florice. I recollect the Master say 'the world would hate you if He changed yo' name,' that's what I recollect."

Florice's shoulders began to shake and she covered her eyes with her hands. It was the crack in the door. Alice walked around the bed quickly and put her arms around her friend and rocked and rocked and rocked. "Now ain't you got a right to the tree of life, huh?" she said softly. "No matter what that man's gone and done." And then she began to sing. "Ain't you got a right to the tree of life, ain't you got a right to the tree of life? Tell my mother, ain't you got a right? Tell my Father, ain't you got a right, ain't you got a right to the tree of life?" She would hold her through the night until the crying was done.

Florice slept as if in a coma. Alice unwound her large arms from around her and set out to do what her memory had told her was needed. She took the pieces of the doll she had dropped in the kitchen and piled them up on the table, carefully looking to see that she had all the hair. Then she went into the parlor and looked through any drawers she saw for white candles. There ought to be plenty, all the formal dinners Florice had had in that house for college girls practicing to be ladies. She found two long candles and placed them in silver candle holders, one on each side of the still recognizable doll. She was reluctant to touch the doll at all, but she would have to take it all apart. She quickly undid Florice's stitches and piled up what was left between the candles. Now she must find the Bible. Time was going fast. It was always by the bed, but maybe there was an extra one in the parlor. She lit the candles and began to pray quickly but intensely, asking God to heal Florice and to make the awful deed powerless. She asked that this "doll" be returned to dust as harmless and she read Florice's favorite passage, St. Paul's letter on charity.

There wasn't much time. She must bury the pieces of the doll in a neutral place. The vacant lot behind the library would do. Florice had always loved the chinaberry tree for its brilliant orange berries so Alice had planted one for her near the dining hall where they spent so many hours together. It was Monday morning, students would be leaving for their holiday soon, but at 7:00, only those hardy souls working morning shift would be up. She saw nobody as she pulled up the softest, youngest root and cut a large piece off. Her hands were steady now. She patted the root back in the ground and thought, It must be 7:15. The fish market opens at 7:30. Alice pulled into her coat tightly and turned the collar up, wrapping her scarf around her head and neck, starting out to walk the two miles to town. She bought a half-pound of mussels, and because she was worried that Florice would wake up and find her gone, was glad to see the bus that would take her most of the way back to campus.

She was still sleeping. But tossing, calling names of people Alice didn't know, snatches of prayers and strange Creole chants. She was feverish. Alice hurried down to the kitchen, almost stumbling on the last step. She washed the chinaberry root and cleaned the mussel shells, throwing the living part away. Then she boiled the shells and root, until she was satisfied the brew tasted vile enough.

Every three hours she would wake Florice as much as she could. And every three hours she would pour the brew down her and hold her head, Florice wretching, and vomiting up what Alice was afraid to look at. The first time she had looked. After that for the entire day and a half while the vomiting went on, she hid her eyes. The stuff was horrible, streaked with black, and it looked alive with something, something Alice didn't want to remember.

It was Tuesday night. Alice had not been home since Sunday afternoon. In the early hours of Wednesday morning, Florice's fever broke. She awoke, as if from a long dream. There was such a deep silence in her, she felt startled almost as if she had been returned from some unknown place, another realm, another reality, and had been put here, a traveler in a strange place, but at peace within her strangeness. Her mouth was chapped and tasted bitter with some foreign taste she didn't recognize. She felt light, light as talcum powder floating on the surface of her bed. It took a while for her eyes to see in the dark night. There was a starchy odor, someone had changed her sheets, and the pillowslips smelled of the sun. For a little while she lay there in such profound peace and relief that it wasn't necessary to remember why she was there. That there was no pain was the overwhelming truth of the moment. And then she began to remember and cry silently, covering her face in revulsion for what she had done, and in horror at what she had willed. There was in her heart the most crushing of all sadnesses, that at having let herself down. She kept whispering "sorry . . . sorry . . ." and used the back of her hand to wipe her face. Gradually she felt someone's presence in the dark room. It spread out and over her like a sweet electricity and though she knew herself to be alone, she was not by herself. The energy surrounded her, lifted her with its Light and set her down in a place of wonder far away from her scream with no bottom. And, while she continued to weep, she knew that somewhere in her deep grief joy was still alive, and as Alice would say, "all is well for true, Florice, all is well. It stands so."

The bagworm moths are best known for the cases the larvae spin around themselves. They carry them wherever they go, and enlarge them as they grow. The adult bagworm is wingless and never feeds but only serves in her

*reproductive function to help the species survive. The bur-
net moths manufacture a poison which circulates in their
blood, helping them to survive the attack of many hostile
organisms.*

1941

"Yo' daddy and me, we wasn't gonna do nothin' either, gurl, back in 1923. No, we was just foolin' round, we was. We wasn't ready for marriage, wasn't thinkin' of no marriage. Till I got you." Alice shook her head. "You hear what I tell you, gurl, it's more'n a notion wih these men! You hear what I tell you."

"Mama, ain't no boy gonna do nothin' to me. I ain't pretty nohow."

Alice thought how young girls could be so blind to how much men saw, and to what they themselves were dying to do.

Maye sulked and was silent. Alice folded clothes and thought about her past, about her shock that she was pregnant, and about Florice's eyes that day back in 1923, when she told Alice that Willie Houston had left town. Alice had only said, "Well, shit, I guess I got me a baby." And the friends had worked it out together. What to tell folks; all of it. She was working as a maid in Jacksonville. They really didn't care that she was expecting a baby. She was just another nigger woman. Another loose nigger woman. Strong as mules they were. Everybody knew that. Alice remembered the leg cramps and how she'd mop and cry, mop and cry and curse Willie Houston. She had never really wanted him. It was all true, you sure would reap what you sowed. She knew she didn't want him at the time, only everybody at church was goin' on in the kitchen about how Willie Houston was sweet on Alice. Even Florice was grinnin' and makin' over her. Alice's good sense went on vacation, she reckoned. Willie Houston worked at the train station. He made a good living and her head began to spin with dreams of a home that was decent and all that other nonsense that had brought so much misery to the world everywhere. Willie Houston wore a sharkskin suit that gleamed in the sun and when he came calling, he wore a black Stetson with a white silk band around it. It was her only adventure. And she had never been scared of nothin' much. Maybe that's what made her act a fool, not bein' scared of enough.

Maye got tired of sitting and walked out the front door. The sound of the door slamming brought Alice back to herself.

"Mind whut I say! Don't you be smat wid me, gurl!" She snapped a large towel, folded it, and laid in on a huge stack of clean laundry.

1941

Eugene Smith had a new master's degree and a new job, principal of Carver school. Mattie thought she ought to have a maid, but Eugene was adamant about the expense, so she sighed and thought of the white school teachers' wives and dusted a little less often. If it couldn't be perfect, there wasn't a lot of point. She went shopping as much as she could and bought as much as she could. There were no children. Those awful children who went to Eugene's school—what if theirs turned out like that? What if they had a child with those really thick lips, and matted, nappy hair? She had been careful to marry a man whose mouth was small, she thought with pride; it was very close to looking like Van Johnson's mouth; and then that terrible cousin showed up, and every time she thought of him being related to Eugene, she cringed. Well, you just couldn't check out everybody in the family, could you? She had explained that to her mother who didn't seem to be comforted. "You don't know what might come up," she said. "I never expected your brother to be as dark as he is. I mean, look at your father, who would've thought it!" And what would she do with a black daughter with nappy hair? No thanks, thought Mattie, I've got enough worries. She turned her head from side to side checking her edges and her brown cheeks. If only that bleaching cream would work before the prom so she could make a good showing for Eugene. Anyhow Mama should have been satisfied. The man had a master's degree. What more did she want from her?

It had happened on a Friday, at 3:15 P.M. School was out. Once more life was to be lived. Good or bad, it was living, not waiting. Girls twittered in bunches, terrified and ecstatic at the raunchy smell of maleness on the other side of the street. Peaches saw them from the window of the bus before she got off. She transferred here from the west side on her way home from work. She shifted her shopping bag to the other sweaty hand. The bag was full of leftover baked chicken and artichoke dressing, which she hated but took anyway, and an unopened can of crabmeat which she had slipped in just because it was easy to do that and get away with it. She had also brought her house slippers, her uniform, and a huge full pocketbook.

The boys were ripe, eager for prey, and needing a victim. Peaches was a match for them, and she enjoyed pulling their strings. "Hey, Peaches, you carry yo' mama in that greasy bag?"

"Yo' mama twice as fat as you!"

"Hey! Robert say he wanta go home wid you . . . he say he want . . ." Laughter, full of the real desire just to see one of those great tits uncovered. It ran the length of the school parking lot and stopped in front of Mattie Smith, and Miss Johnson, eighth grade teacher, on their way to the cars and walking toward the flag pole.

Miss Letitia Johnson knew these youngsters well. She was not afraid of them, but she was terrified that the principal's wife would discover that Letitia Johnson was from "the grove," and could talk about anybody's mother like an expert if need be. The Letitia Johnson who had been in disguise for six years. That Letitia Johnson did not have a teaching job or a young man studying at the college. Her ears were hot around the edges.

"Hey mama . . . you, Peaches . . . Miz Johnson, she say you done caused the last flood when you sit in the tub . . . and Miz Smith she say yo' daddy a ole white man, and she say yo' mama a big black ho!"

They were almost at the flag pole. But Peaches had just realized she had never before been challenged in front of a twenty-three year old underdone schoolmarm. This would be like sucking tender meat from between rib bones.

The girls were silently waiting. Doomsday had been announced and there was nowhere to run. The boys, who were too far away for identification, melted into the trees, strutted and tasted the disaster. Someone said, ''Ooh, Miz Smith gon get them . . . OOOH . . .'' and then Peaches met Miss Johnson and Mrs. Smith when they reached the flagpole. They were close enough to see each other's eyelashes, to smell each others smells. At this distance there were no secrets. Peaches enjoyed it all. Gathering saliva from the corners behind where her teeth had been, she sucked in her cheeks, and spat twice, once on each face. Miss Johnson was frantically fumbling for her handkerchief and her books which she had dropped all over the sidewalk, when she heard Mrs. Smith's high-pitched voice. It came twisting twisting through her ears from one side of her head to the other. ''You goddamned cow! You ain't nothin' but yellow wasted! How you come to be half white anyhow!'' Peaches threw back her head in a toothless triumph and Letitia grabbed Mattie's hand in mid-slap. Somehow swimming through the laughter, they managed to get into the car and drive off, spraying Peaches with red clay dust.

Mattie Smith wiped the saliva off her cheek with Letitia's hanky. As she threw it out into the street with a shudder, the tears began to roll down her face. There was a visible stain under each arm of Letitia's new blouse. She remembered her books. She'd have to put in a requisition for some new ones on Monday.

They hated her for her bodacious fat and her refusal to excuse it. They hated her for being proud of her white ladies and for not complaining, with them, that there was just so much white folks would dish out and then you had to sit down on the job and have a smoke. Peaches never shared her hidden corners of rebellion, she never talked about ''them,'' wanted to walk off the job, or spit in the food she fried. As far as they knew, she never stole a teaspoon of liquor or food from her ''white ladies.''

Most of the neighborhood hated Peaches enough to leave her isolated, but feared her enough to know she would have you, have you all, if she was messed with. The ''hinckty'' colored folks tried to ignore her. The ''common niggers'' tried to joke about her. Neither group was very successful.

Mrs. Stevens, her "white lady," said she'd never had a better cook, and Peaches agreed; she hadn't. The last lady she worked for was found without one hand that Thursday that Peaches took off to go look for her lost nephew. She was found slung across the washboard in the basement with a rag wrapped around the stump and they never found the hand. Peaches was really broken up about "her white lady" who never said a mean word to her all the time she was workin' there and who saw to it she got the best of all the kitchen leftovers. Peaches was so upset she came and just sat on Miss Lady's porch and the tears rolled down her fat face all day. Miz Stephens had seen her lady that very day and had seen Peaches too, laughin' and jokin' about how she had to run down her lost nephew and it was a shame 'bout younguns these days, and she left her lady alive and well at 2:00 P.M. with Miz Stephens right there at the house.

"They said they were white," she told Florice, "but really they're Jewish." "Same as white," Florice had said. "They not *colored*, they're *white*. Ain't nothin' else in this land." Peaches was always bringing home what they didn't want or need, to feed her own empty space in the long evening. But she never stole a crumb, never.

It was after the younguns had told her to do that thing that day. It was after that day she had heard the squirrels.

She had enjoyed it all, but then something happened. The plants twisted when she got home, leaning toward her, whispering that they had seen. They danced in the afternoon light, crawled toward her, running their green fingers through her fingers, laughing the same pealing laughter, the same yaah yaah, and finally, their spit landed in her hair.

She stood in front of the mirror examining her tremendous body. It suited her to be fat; someone had once called her a mountainous woman. She smiled. Well, they'd see if she couldn't be a woman all right, in spite of, no maybe because of her hills and valleys of fat. She'd have her ass and his too. Peaches took a look at the ripples of flesh; she was familiar with the every pore and she hated herself into being what she was—like wallowing in herself, like stuffing herself with a despised food just because maybe, maybe if she got enough of it, food would lose its great power. She ran her hand over one great breast and down her side where there should have been a waist. "Don't need nobody's waist," she said to herself. "Been a long time since I took somebody on." There were pocked marks of light brown flesh and great puffed feet that stuck out under the lip of her leg which rolled jellylike, almost covering the ankle.

She dressed herself in an oversized pair of denim coveralls and a huge lumber-jacket shirt that made of her more of a balloon man than anything. Her hair was wispy, half-white hair, short and ash-brown and dirty. A pair of tennis shoes, incongruously clean, seemed to squeak onto her feet. There were no underclothes in her house.

Stepping out into the afternoon, she made her way down the porch steps carefully. She knew it would go hard with her to break any bones and she had a stiff leg. Nobody remembered how she got that, not even Peaches. The sun was glancing towards the west, pale shots of sun, bright but not warm. Her shadow moved like a rubber cloud; solid, determined, and not once did it occur to her that there was another way to be.

Twice, she thought, it'll have to be twice. Had no business sayin that to anybody, anybody. What I hear, I hear. Squirrels had whispered it to her the other night. Squirrels never lied. They knew. They bit hard and they knew.

Three of them, dark spots on a sea of purple. And hot rain. Falling into their necks and on their bare arms and Florice was pushing, pushing the great sea back but it wouldn't stay put. No matter where she put the water, it wouldn't stay. There were buckets and buckets of purple and red water she kept emptying them on the land and then the spots appeared on the beach. Her feet were melting, she was losing, and the shadows were taking over. One shadow opened and screamed and then another and then suddenly there were rows and rows and rows of schoolchildren dressed in black and a Black man dressed in black but his face was gray and in each of his hands were two peaches.

Florice woke up, jerking her head back and forth across the pillow. She turned on the light and sat up. My Lord, my Lord. She breathed quietly. It was 4:30 A.M. Peaches, it had ended with peaches. She closed her eyes again with the light on, fully awake, but in deep concentration.

There were telephone poles, pine trees glancing in and out of the sun. This great body walked among them as a reality, not to be a part of grace, but to be acknowledged even so. To be paid homage to, just for its bulk alone. To be reckoned with, to be paid attention to, to be even honored. Florice heard her own fear, and the large silent footsteps. She took hold of this human soul because it planted itself in her path and would not be moved. Here am I. Peaches. Not to be a thing with, but a thing apart, my own, my self, like a mountainous reminder that there are those cursed by knowing that they are hungry, but not knowing that they are empty.

About 5:45 she looked up and saw the great bulk of Peaches picking its way through the sun spots on the sidewalk. It was time. Where she would begin she didn't know. She didn't know where Peaches was going either, but she had been given information about her destination—that it would mean trouble for others and that a person who needed was coming. She stepped out on her porch. "Why, hello, Peaches. How you this afternoon?" Florice took her time, not too friendly, but interested, interested.

Peaches stopped, looked up. Florice was examining her porch swing with apparent great interest in the state of the white paint and rust.

"How you do, ma'am, Miss Florice," she answered.

"How you like this weather, Peaches?"

"Most tolerable, Miss Florice, most tolerable." She started to take another step when something in the woman's smile and the unusual greeting directed her to stop (though it was not unusual for Miss Florice, she thought, 'cause she spoke to everybody). Something had her feeling she wanted to stop, so she forgot about the squirrels and what they had said, for a few minutes.

"Come up for somethin' hot? Peaches?"

She took her hands out of her pockets and slowly made her feet step toward the lady, who, though different, was certainly a lady.

It wasn't in what they said. They talked of preserves and

of pickles. They talked of working for white folks and of how awful it was to be almost at war, and of young folks who should know better than to do what they do. It was in the light that shone from the slightly odd lady, who could see that a hungry person will eat three times what she needs, and do God knows what else to make life seem livable.

Then Peaches brought up the squirrels. "They talk," she said. "And they done tole me that them Smiths been talkin' 'bout me behind my back and I should do somethin' 'bout it." Florice didn't blink an eye. She had had her own experiences with hearing things talk. We didn't all hear the same voices.

"That so, Peaches?"

"Yes, ma'am, and they say I need to get my satisfaction. Folks talkin' 'bout me. It ain't right, callin' me names, they is—ole half-white fatso and such like. Yes ma'am, they is." She twisted and the chair almost tipped over.

Her concentration was not on the words but on the state of the woman. Her voice was dark, slow, and determined. And it covered an anger so deep that it reached into places no one had ever seen. Florice stalked that anger, to feel it, to know it. Where others had seen only the monster, she saw the monster's twin. Peaches' voice came out of an immense cavern. "It ain't right, and I'm gonna teach 'em, it ain't right." The cavern was colored midnight, and Peaches was lost somewhere under layers and layers of fleshly anger. She had picked up a table knife and was fingering the edge. Florice put her coffee cup down. The kitchen was quiet. Somewhere outside, a car radio blasted a Frank Sinatra tune.

"Peaches, you know who those Smiths are?" Florice was searching troubled waters, and wounded creatures will struggle. "They here to help us learn about ourselves."

"How you mean, Miss Florice?"

"Well you know we need people like the Smiths to tell us what *we* supposed to be doin' here sometimes just cause *they* make mistakes. Now, if I tell you to forget about them for a few days, you think you could do that?"

There was a long silence. Florice knew the fish was on the hook. Now it was a matter of playing the line so that she could pull it on in. Their eyes met and broke, and met again.

"What you think about my lady's being killed like that, Miss Florice?" It was not a smile yet, that flickered at her chin, but Florice felt her own skin hum, and she played it carefully, just pull it in gently, she thought, gently, gently.

"I think folks go when their time comes, Peaches. That's what. Gettin' dark. You walkin' home?" She knew Peaches would go home. Today, anyhow. The knife was back on the table next to the butter dish. The great hands were still. The line was slack.

"Let me turn on the porch light. Don't you fall now. Goodnight, Peaches. You have a good night." She languished, like a great whale, and then she swallowed the night.

* * *

Scrubbing was a chore she had always strangely enjoyed. There is no hot like the hot of scrubbing in the heat of summer on your knees. There is no sweat like that that runs down your face as you bend over the bucket. Florice thought of the foot washers' church—no wonder they did that—did everyone good to get down on their knees every once in a while. The scrub brush made that peculiar slurp scratching sound— that sound that sailors on board ship have shared with convent nuns and with those everywhere whose backs have ached. Floors are the lowest of all, but should be clean, she thought, because where your feet walk, there also goes your head. God, ain't that the truth, Florice grunted to herself. Besides, gritty floors made her teeth crawl. She grinned at her own poetry and had just leaned back on her heels to be proud of her work when the screen slammed. It was Maye. "Miss Florice, Miss Florice, Mama say turn on the radio quick! She say white folks gon send us to war again!"

1941

Some said she sucked out the blood and closed up the wound, just like that. Some said it wasn't nothin.' She just cut it and sucked out the blood like everybody knew how to do anyway. But others said she could talk to snakes and they were never sure what happened. Most of the children who saw it were told to "hush up and stop that nonsense." Everybody knew Miss Florice was a nice God-fearin' lady, even if she was a little strange. They would be quiet, but they would always remember and they would pass the story on for at least three generations.

Peetie McPherson would never forget that picnic, he knew what he saw all right, and he would tell his own grandchildren how Durell Thomas had been healed by a witch right there in a park near Greensboro, N.C. "There wasn't too many of us who saw," he would say. "They was Junie Bug and Buck and Bernice his sister, and Taliofarro Brewster and maybe one or two more. And they were all after climbin' them rocks," he would say; "and we had left the grown folks barbecuing and fixin' the dinner. Lord, we had walked a far piece. I wouldn't try to do that now! So we sat down on the nearest thing we could see to set on, you know, and it was some old dead logs piled up in the woods and we was all hot and sweaty like. And little Bernice, she was little and couldn't walk so fast, and she come up saying she was sho tired and ready to go back. And Buck he told her to shut up 'cause sisters do be worryin' ya to death. And just as we got up to go up the big hill we was wanting to climb, Durell, he screamed almighty bloody murder and we saw the snake. Only it was too late for Durell 'cause it had bit him good, a big copperhead. And there we was, with no grown folks, off in the woods a far piece. Bernice was yellin' and half crazy, and the rest of us just didn't know what to do and that snake just slid on off; I reckon we was too many to fight. We was all up on the log, holdin' on to each other and Durell just screamin' 'I'm dead, I'm dead, the snake done bit me, I'm dead.' Well sir, Junie Bug, he took off with everybody behind him but me, I stayed to help Durell die, I reckon. And 'bout half mile out they run into that lady Miss Florice, who said, 'Y'all all come with me' and, 'Anybody got a knife?' and Junie Bug he have a pocket knife and he give it to her.

"Durell, he had got real quiet by the time they all come back there where he was. He was just cryin' quiet and callin' for his mama. And then up come Miss Florice, and she say 'Durell, Durell you hear me? You be all right, you be all right!' and then she say, 'Y'all, Junie and Peetie, hold him down'; and she say, 'This here's gonna hurt you, Durell, but it'll save your life.' And she take the knife, and she cut around that bite and Durell screamin', and Miss Alice holdin' the younguns back and I saw blood spurtin' out and like to took sick. And Durell, he passed out. Then she bent over Durell and sucked on that cut and spit out the poison. Never have seen a woman with that much nerve, before or since." And then he would pause, and look at his grandchildren, and they would all get ready for this part, knowing that it was the best part. "And then," he would say, dramatically, "she put her hands on Durell's leg where that snake done bit him, and he done been cut, and she closed her eyes and you could see her mouth was saying something quiet, and when she tuk her hands away, and here's my hand to God, when she tuk her hands away, the snakebite had disappeared! It wasn't no blood, no cut, nor nothin'!" And the children would be satisfied for another summer, and Peetie McPherson would remember how he tried to tell his folks and everybody, and nobody believed him except those children who were there and Junie Bug who was a wild child and not to be trusted anyhow. And then when Durell fainted, of course, they had to send for his folks and the doctor and all, and carry him out of the woods and the grown folks just took over asking questions, but they only asked Miss Alice and Miss Florice, who said something about an insect bite and maybe he should be checked at the hospital. And everybody was telling the children they was hysterical and to just be quiet. Peetie would remember how he had tried to tell about the snake bite and the awful cutting, but they just shut him up, and Junie Bug left his knife to rust in the woods and that was the only evidence. In fifty years he would remember how Miss Florice walked back to the picnic with him and Junie Bug, and before they reached the tables she had said, "Well boys, you know how folks are. Suppose we just keep this one a secret, okay? Look like they don't want to believe you anyhow." And she had smiled and patted them on the shoulder and walked away with Miss Alice.

* * *

The afternoon was heavy with threatening thunderstorms. She was in a deep woods and her head was wet with sweat. Over and over again she was being asked to heal people, hundreds of people lined up in rows, all wailing and calling for help. There was no way, no way she would ever have the strength to do it and then there were more and more people staring at her, looking hostile, suspicious and scornful. "Go on, let's see you do it," they were saying. Some were saying she was of the devil and some were on their knees praying, and all of them looked like angry animals. Their faces were elongated and their eyes were accusing. There were some that held snakes high over their heads, and the snakes began to call to her, "Sister, sister." And they began to writhe and shake and she could hear rattlers and they held up their hands and there were rattlers in their open palms.

A storm was gathering and there was nowhere to escape so she started healing them, one by one, until somebody screamed, "Devil child, devil woman," and she began to run, her hair streaming behind her and her legs twisting under her. Rain was coming down hard now, she could see nothing but walls of rain, and then it was there, abruptly, but the only way to get in was through a glass door which was sealed shut. She pounded and pounded on and on, until through the glass she saw him dressed in his robes for Sunday service. She rammed her fists into the door, again and again, but he went on working, bent over his books which seemed carved of ice, and his desk was ice, and the walls and the furniture, and then she realized that Robert was also sculptured in ice. She stopped pounding. The only movement and the only color in the entire room was the rush of red blood through his veins.

1942

Harriet was coming in on the eleven-thirty train from Chicago. It had been four years since Dr. Benedict had told her she would have to leave Centenary College because of her "unfortunate situation," and three and a half years since Ronald had come home on furlough to marry her. Now he was somewhere in North Africa and Harriet was the mother of a little girl whose father was fighting in a war. Harriet had never made it back to school, and had worked the four years to keep herself and Ronnie. Florice's sister had been nice to her, but Harriet felt herself a burden, and her mama had said before she died, "never be a burden to anyone if you can help it." So, she found a job cleaning in a kitchenette in Bronzeville. She still had hopes of going to school and maybe someday she would be a college graduate. The state school had accepted her application and she had written to tell Florice. She had never stopped writing Florice, Ronnie's godmother.

"Hard work has been good to you, honey." Florice was really glad to see Harriet; she had never ceased being fond of her first "student in trouble," and was really overjoyed to see the baby. "Well, Lord have mercy, this must be Ronnie!" She was scooping her up in a half-second in her strong arms. "You just don't mean it! A little doll baby!" Ronnie's eyes were bright and a bit wider than usual. Just who was this expansive lady who had picked her up so fast and who had not even asked her mother for permission to do so? "Well, Lord, let's get her in from this night air. It's been real damp today. We can't have you sick now, can we?" The luggage was slim and the conversation soon turned to a job and Harriet's father who was failing and how long this war would go on. Harriet felt at home at last. It had taken her a long time to forget that Chevy truck disappearing down the street. She would not have to dream that dream again.

She put herself in the bed, a weary muscle at the time. To work so hard should have some reward, Rebecca thought, as the blood tingled inside her calves and across her hips. Slowly she realized this was to be one of these nights when she was too tired to find the black peace of sleep. Images of people floated in and out of her view—Mac, Mama, Theodore. They all lived in her head constantly. She had always wondered why the human brain didn't just break down and refuse to function loaded with so much stuff, and it seemed hers never stopped moving, forever turning, turning; if it was not what to do about some nuisance problem, it was how to solve somebody's troubles. The blackness whirled and faces floated up from some basement level to meet her. Why couldn't they leave her be at night, faces, and then ugliness. She tossed until the sheets were twisted—like a shroud she thought. Uncomfortable thoughts crowded in as if to haunt, demon doubts. What if God wasn't really there, but only her frantic hope, so she wouldn't be alone in her strangeness? So many times she had heard folks talking about how some people didn't really believe in God but just wouldn't admit it. Maybe God was a cheat and there was no real reason to love anybody except yourself. A cheat, a cheat. There was a comet in her darkness. It twisted with her blanket and suddenly she saw the face of Alice Wine in agony, swirling around with the comet. It flashed through her head and left a deep blackness.

In the midnight of her room, she was wide awake. She opened her eyes wide and then closed them again quickly as if to shut out Alice's face. Not that, not a message about Alice. Rebecca shook her head to slough off the image. She thought she'd open the window, maybe the air would put her to sleep. First she heard the crickets and then the birds. Robert had said, when birds sing at midnight, "It's God's lullabye."

The hidden places—the inside, what could be hidden on the inside, with the roots going deep into the earth? Maybe that's what she really was, she thought, an old hollow tree rooted to the ground, dusty and ancient and twisted, trying with it all to reach, reach, until she risked snapping those old fibers. Maybe her heart would snap too but really she didn't fear that anymore—what it had endured, her heart. What it had endured. To love all and nothing, no one and yet everyone all at the same time—to have lost all and found nothing . . . to have belonged to no one and everyone; the roots cannot snap, the heart cannot break that is both empty and full at the same time for that tree reaches both ways into it all—all the way into it all.

She had walked down some rocky roads, but the thought of not having Alice to help carry the load was not admissible, it was just not admissible. "God's lullabye. Must mean something good," she thought. And then she slept, quickly.

1942

Maye went out about three o'clock for her evening at the local movie house. Harriet said selling popcorn in the colored section wasn't the best job in the world 'cause all manner of common people come in and out of that place, especially for some of those movies no real God-fearing person would go to see, but Maye said she needed the money and besides it got her out of the house for a while and she was restless as a cat without her kittens in the summertime. Anyway, Miss Alice Wine said the girl was in her late teens, and anything she had taught her would have to take by now or it never would.

That evening wasn't particularly hot, just overcast for July and full of insects and mosquitoes brought out by the rain, and folks were tired of the grayness that week had brought. One of those days when you'd just as soon summer was winter.

Maye was a peculiar girl, even then, sweet and kind of touchy at the same time. She was much older than Ronnie was so she didn't know her too well, only remembered how sorry she was for her for the rest of her life.

But that day she remembered because of the excitement in her house and because everybody tried to hush up in front of her. She was old enough to know that if Mama sent her out to weed the garden, or up to her room to play, especially if Miss Florice came in with that serious look, that meant there was surely something happening that she wasn't supposed to know about except she did.

Maye left home, Harriet said later, with that kind of vacant look she often had, dressed in a flowered skirt, little red flowers with yellow stems. After that nobody knew exactly what happened because the next person to see her was Miss Florice and he had already taken the light from Maye's eyes that would never come back.

From sun to sun there stretches a hurt that never lets itself be felt all the way. It broke through the quiet of the girl's movements, so that in years to come she would jerk involuntarily, almost having forgotten why she did it. The way she jerked when he finally forced it in her.

When he came into the supply room where she was filling those bags with popcorn, all she could smell was the popcorn and sweat and all she could think was If he touches me I'll vomit all over the popcorn, and the thought made her even sicker. "Miss Maye, you give old Bubba some sugar now, he ain't so bad as all that." He had said it, thinking she would kick or at least scratch, but none of that happened. She remembered the hair on his arms and the sound of Donald O'Connor's singing in the rain coming through the speaker. They must have been at the part where Gene Kelly was splashing in the puddles when she decided that if she moved from the corner behind the cleaning supplies she would not be sick in the popcorn but it covered it covered the whole world those big white puffy kernels those bags of dust would open and cover her legs with dripping running corn, she couldn't wipe it off, she couldn't find the door she had to get somewhere away from the whiteness and she'd lose her job and she was falling falling slipping—there were too many people who would tell it was her fault of course it was her fault she couldn't stop him and she would lose her job and no one would believe that she was smothered by the white mountain that stuck its hugeness between her painful . . .

Who is Alice Wine's daughter? Who was/is beauty young and open love sweet bunch of plum blossom bruised that never heals (in a blossom) in whose book do you press a flower that will never look the same? Press her in a book of sorrow who is Alice Wine's daughter who was plum and purple love who was going to be fruit who was going to be rich who was going to be plum wine.

The doorbell rang in that weak way someone rings who is

not sure they have the right house. Florice put down her Louisiana teacup aware that the tea would be cold when she finally picked it up again. She knew immediately that the ring wasn't right, and went to the door reluctantly, not wanting to face serious hassle today. Through the sheers at the door, she saw a young woman vaguely familiar, the outline of her profile painful even at a distance. When she got to the fern pot she could see who it was, and the realization, like the doorbell, went down to that place in her stomach lining where she always felt death scratching.

"Mama say. . . ," she said it so low her voice came through her skin rather than through her mouth, "Mama say . . . you let those men touch you down there, you'll never be no good, she said . . . you'll never be no good no more . . ."

Florice led her toward the kitchen table, had to force herself to look away from the bloodstains on the skirt. "Here, got some hot herb tea. See my African violets? How they've grown this year. Sit down now . . . let's see, a piece of toast?" She was holding the girl's hand lightly, looking steadily at her, as if by her will she could stop the scream which she knew was forcing its way through Maye's drowning eyes. After that day she never again thought of the odor of semen with pleasure.

With every circle made by the phone numbers the sickness grew, until she thought out loud Why this one, Lord, why and what do I do with my anger, some of it to you, Lord, some of it, and the sickness turned toward herself as she all at the same time thought how her energy must go in the child's direction quickly quickly push the sickness back and think of her and Alice. It rang and rang and Florice wickedly thought Maybe she won't be home and I don't really have to tell her and she answered. Florice's voice had that depth it took on when she was really frightened. "Alice, that you? Maye's over here and I think you'd best come." Alice knew, by the elastic stretch in her friend's voice that strained from the soles of Rebecca's feet and sounded as if it were pulling her hair out at the roots. Alice knew her time for suffering had come. She knew too that Rebecca Florice was there like the dirt was there in the garden, like the Baptist church was there in the South, that her friend was there. She walked slowly, knowing that whatever it was it wouldn't change by her rushing to meet it.

Florice put down the phone slowly and even more slowly dialed Dr. George's number. "Right now . . . it'll keep. Just get here, please."

Gently she guided Maye toward the bed. "You just rest now; your mama will be here soon!" She hesitated and then removed the reddened skirt gently, folded it and put it aside for the doctor. Not that they would need to see it. Maye was plucking at her stained slip with little jerks, and tears had finally started to run slowly down her cheeks. She began to tremble, "But, but . . . it was everywhere and I fell, I fell, I fell."

Alice had come up the steps slowly, with the weight of sorrow tied to each foot. She sat Maye in the hot bath as if asleep, and poked at the burning clothes, as the fire ate up her insides.

Folks said she never woke up all the way again. That sleep-walkin' girl, they called her. She began to feel the eyes of men on her everywhere. They knew, she knew, and their eyes followed her. She had a way of rubbing her hips as if she felt a spot there. One day, one came to her house. Her mama had finally taken her home, had said folks would begin to talk about why they had just picked up and moved, so they went back home, and then Alice began to notice how much sleeping Maye was doing. She had been right. Maye would never be the same, and a brittle plum blossom never smells sweet again.

One came to her house and Maye was home alone. She was rarely alone anymore; she would tremble until Alice came back, and Alice had agreed only to go out when Mama Carrie was next door. Maye was afraid when she heard the knock on the door, but there was only the screen and he could see her sitting at the kitchen table. "Hey gal," he said, "how's about it? Pay you. Pay you good. A dollar fifty?" His pink fatness spread like a cancer around her and she decided that day that she was going to hell. What really mattered anymore? What really mattered? As soon as Alice and Florice topped the porch steps, they knew the smell of whiskey and cigar smoke. The bedroom door was slightly ajar, and the old iron bed had squeaked when Alice had gotten Maye and when Alice had birthed Maye.

Alice's voice sounded down the corridors of heaven and hell in a cracking sob and she began to break her best plates, that were stacked up on the kitchen table. Pieces of chipped china fell around them, bounced off the white enameled table. Finally Rebecca took both her hands and called to her, "Alice, Alice girl, don't do that, don't."

"But she gone, Florice, she gone now, she gone." On and on and on, the word sounded. Final is never final because it never leaves us in peace because it is final, because it is not ever final.

Later that night, Maye looked down at the dollar and fifty cents in her hand and stared out the kitchen window. Garbage needs takin' out, she thought, and pulled the window shut.

At dawn, Rebecca took out her box, for remembrance, for the love of the look and feel of her things. They reminded her of the old days, of Mac and Theodore, and they reminded her of what was to come. A piece of polished granite she loved to hold; the sand dollar from Bear Island, shells and a dried flower; natural wool from sheep and some strange wooden shapes she had found along the road on one of her walks, the butterfly, the beetle.

She felt them all, one by one, gently handling the tissue around the butterfly. It was foolish to open the paper and touch it. The black wings would turn to powder with the slightest pressure. She held the sand dollar in her hand loving its incomplete roundness, its half-mystical markings, wondering who first made up the story about the sand dollar representing the wounds of Christ. She wanted someday to find a whole one, if she ever got back to the coast, a complete sand dollar, intact, with all its wounds visible. She wanted to feel it—the energy of life, the love of it all, in those pieces of the world in her box. She needed the strength that comes with knowing the things of the earth.

Ole Bubba lived in a shotgun house out near the edge of

the state college farm. He was the kind who kept money in mattresses, and who kept "the other niggers in line" at the movie. The owner of the theater thought he'd be perfect to have around and see that the girls he hired didn't steal the ticket or refreshment money at the colored section. He was perfect. He enjoyed his work.

Rebecca remembered where the house was. She took her umbrella out of the stand near the door and put on her gardening shoes to walk in. Her eyes were twin stones. They hardened, solidified into purpose as she picked up a solid gnarled branch and put her umbrella back.

One, two, three, four, a rhythm as regular as a working man's hammer, as if she were made of metal, catching him at the depths of a wine-induced sleep. He never broke the silence of the dawn. The only noises in the old shack came from her wooden branch and the magnificent sunrise. She had cracked four bones before she snatched her anger back from death.

Slowly, walking slowly with the branch of hickory. She passed the farm where college boys experimented with cattle and pigs. Lean some forward, picking her way around gravel and twigs, forward to whatever had to be done next. The fields were beautiful with September wildflowers. Queen Anne's lace, delicate white, too white for Florice. She suddenly preferred the dandelion's bright yellow. It had more spunk, it was *there* not here or maybe, but really present and accounted for. She was present. Was she accounted for? That Queen Anne's lace was what it was and would be, and would be. Maye was what Maye was. She stopped at the pasture fence and was reminded that four-footed creatures do well with their decisions. Four-footed wisdom would have allowed Bubba to rest in his fat until it grew rancid of its own accord. She sighed heavily.

"Hey, Miss Florice, ma'am, how you?" The vegetable man passed on his way to cry the streets about "fresh greens and maters," and tipped his straw hat. "Out mighty early this morning aren't you?" His mule paused and she declined a ride on the wagon by the unspoken tilt of her head. "Just taking my morning walk.'' She rested her stick against the fence casually.

"Well, good day, ma'am," he said, curiously. Florice was thankful for his good sense. She walked off quickly. She had decided to give Ronnie the stone from her box she had slipped into her pocket that morning before light.

Ronnie was playing at mudpies in the backyard. The dandelions were serving as her main course, as dessert, as everything except the biscuits which were, of course, the mudpies. "Hi, Miss Florice," she said absentmindedly. "Mama's in the kitchen. What you come for, breakfast?" Florice winced. Even a four-year old baby seemed to be aware of her strange morning walk.

"Nope, come to give you something. You got a box belongs to you? You can put things in?" Ronnie thought a long time. "Yep, be right back." Her little back was resolute with purpose. Now of course, not knowing what the box was for didn't matter to her. Miss Florice asked for a box, that must be what she wants. Florice heard Harriet say, "Girl, look at them hands!" and realized she had sent Ronnie in the house at the wrong time. Ronnie must have used her considerable wit because she was back in a flash with the box she had been given to keep pencils in and said, "Here,"—stretching her short arms out fast and turning just as fast to answer calls of, "Just come right back here and wash your hands!"

When she returned with hands much too clean to play in the mud, Florice was tickled that Ronnie still had not told her mother that Florice was there. Harriet was somewhere doing what women always had to do, glad that Ronnie was occupying herself. Ronnie was aware with some part of her, that Miss Florice was different from all the ladies who came to visit her mama. She liked her with her four years because she made good cookies and she liked her with the shadow of unnumbered years that she couldn't yet listen to. She felt it in the hands of the lady, in the warm way her hair felt, after Florice smoothed it, in the eyes that said here is safety, here is truly home. There was a circle which she wanted to step into with Florice, even at four, and she knew Miss Florice knew, even though she could only say, "She makes good cookies."

"Feel this," Florice said, reaching forward with the rock. It was a smooth stone with a deep crevice through one side. Worn, as it had been rubbed clean by the rain for many years. "Nice," Ronnie said with wide eyes. "Now I want you to put this in your treasure box and keep it."

"But why?"

"Because someday you will need to know how to be hard and soft at the same time." And so you will not forget how, she said in a whisper to herself. Ronnie put the rock carefully in her pencil box, looked thoughtfully at Miss Florice, and then Harriet said, her head poking around the back door, "And what y'all up to? What you doin' here, girl, this early? Come in, for heaven's sake, and have some coffee. You off today? Ronnie, put your pencil box up. Go on now, do as Mama says. You off today?"

"I *took* off today. Had business to tend to." Florice tried to shake off the memories of sound as she drank her coffee with Harriet. "Ever had any bone china, Florice?" Harriet scowled at the chip in her grocery store blue and white cup and saucer.

Hickory wood cracking bone. She had almost succeeded. Morning sound of September birds, the junk man's truck and jump rope chant on the front sidewalk Mack dressed in black/silver buttons all down her back/drink my coffee drink my tea "Drink your coffee, girl" for it gets cold all around the neighborhood talk about me, me, me, bone you know they call it that if it's made in England one had a roastin ear tied roun his neck. Pushed out her chair. "Got to go." "You sick, Florice?" Two small feet hit the pavement over and over again. Hickory stick you ain't sick come on Dinah you ain't sick all you need is a hickory stick just a history stick just a hickory stick. She forgot. Almost. Left it by that fence.

Moths and butterflies cannot physically resist attacks with strong jaws, hard shells, or poison stings as insects of other orders do. Their appearance, shape, and color of-

ten enable them to escape the notice of enemies and deceive their opponents. Very important are adaptations of form and color that enable them to mislead.

1942

War was raging on the other side of the world but Alice thought there was no reason it had to be fought on her back stoop and she made her way from the front bedroom through the small kitchen of her rented house. "Smells of coal in here," she said to no one. It was a frost-biting day and Alice had been in bed most of the day, in front of her coal stove in the room she called a front bedroom but which was really a former dining room. It had served as that at one time and still had the pretension of glass French doors that she had curtained with cream-colored rayon because it gave her some privacy.

Damn war was everywhere, in her stomach and on her own back stoop. Alice picked up a useless old rusty spoon. "Git! You cats, git. Go fight your pussy battles somewhere else." The spoon hit the tom from next door on the rump but they were very used to Alice's outbursts and the cats only ambled out of her throwing arm's reach as if she were a minor annoyance, much less significant than their struggle over some poor feminine feline destined to have yet another litter. "All over a little piece of tail," Alice muttered. "If we only knew it, this damn war is probably over some woman somewhere."

1943 Thanksgiving

"It ain't no good," she said with a stubborn look that clearly meant there was no persuading her otherwise. "It's not any good," Harriet corrected, as if that would move the child. "This place ain't no good, Mama, and we should go." They had come to watch the Christmas parade. There were crowds of people everywhere waiting for things to start. They had found a good spot in the front and Harriet wondered what could possibly be wrong with Ronnie. When she got her mind stuck on something, she was the devil to be moved. "I wanna go home, Mama, let's go home." Harriet was just dismayed. All the trouble they had gone to to get downtown to this Christmas parade and the Thanksgiving turkey she had had to get up at the crack of dawn to start, so they could come. "I wanna go home!" The tears were starting. They had walked to town, and now they would have to walk back because there would be no buses until after the parade. Harriet saw some of the students from Centenary, and some of the members of her church, but no one looked interested in walking home with a crying five-year-old. She turned and picked Ronnie up. "Listen," she said, shaking her just a little. "Listen. If we go home, that's it. You understand? I am not coming back to town today. You got me all the way here, and I'll take you home, but that's it." Ronnie knew she had pushed her mother to the limit. She shook her head slowly and took in two sharp breaths between sobs. "Okay then, missy, let's go." Harriet set her down firmly and took her by the hand. They started out, the wool ball on Ronnie's blue knit hat bobbing up and down. Harriet's firm steps resolute and resigned, Ronnie occasionally sniffing tears.

The turkey was well on its way. Florice would be there for dinner, and Alice, and she wanted everything nice, but she had to catch her breath a minute from the long walk. Ronnie had stopped crying and was watching her cat. They had both been quiet for a while. "Well," said Harriet aloud, "I'd best get to dinner. Sure wish your daddy was here for the holiday, little one. It's been a long time." She had cried her own tears these long war years. Seemed like Ronald had been gone forever. Now the tears were mostly private, under covers, and late at night, but holidays were as much a curse as a blessing.

It was getting on toward four o'clock. The doorbell rang twice. She had wanted to put her grief away, have a lovely dinner, and count her blessings but she found it wasn't as easy as just deciding to do it. Didn't nobody say it would be easy, she thought, swallowing a lump in her throat. She thought about this afternoon. Maybe Ronnie's tears and confusion were just a mirror of her own struggle with loneliness.

The ladies were dressed in festive colors and smiling. They both carried large dishes that smelled wonderful and the hugs and kisses and teasing were good for Harriet. At least it took her away from Ronald and the war for a while.

Coffee time. Ronnie was standing quietly at the living room window staring into the dark. She heard a fire siren. They had always frightened her. Only recently had she stopped crawling into Harriet's bed after a siren passed. Florice noticed her pensive mood, unusual for a child on a holiday. The women looked at each other, communicating without words. "Want some more ice cream, baby?" Harriet had always thought a good treat would calm anybody's nerves. Ronnie came and sat on Florice's lap hiding her head in her godmother's breast. Florice stroked her hair and looked quietly into Ronnie's face.

"I'm scared of the fire. It's gonna be a fire. I see a fire." Harriet put her fork down. "Where, baby?" Ronnie just shook her head.

"Well, now, you wanna see trouble? How about a story from de island?" Alice could always come up with something magic she remembered from home. "Let's not talk about this ole fire. Maybe you like to hear the story of ole Mr. Alligator who wanna see trouble?'' Ronnie and Alice left the table, Alice holding Ronnie's hand and talking about all the little alligators who slithered into the field, ''kapuk, kapuk, kapuk.''

''What's wrong with her, Florice?'' Harriet leaned her head on her hand. ''Lord, I got enough trouble to carry with Ronald away.''

''I think she can see, Harriet.''

''See? What do you mean?''

''I mean like me.'' She hesitated. ''I think she has the gift. I don't know for sure, but I think so.'' The Thanksgiving candles were burning low on the dining room table. Florice blew them out and the smoke drifted toward the ceiling. Harriet thought of the burden her friend carried, had carried for so long, so alone. She didn't want that for Ronnie. There was something frightening and sad about being able to see the future, about knowing more than most people.

''Oh my God, my baby. What kinda life will she have?''

''She'll be all right, Harriet. She'll be fine. Only whatever you do, don't make her feel like she's crazy.''

The phone rang and startled both of them, they were so deep into their own thoughts. Harriet paled as she replaced the receiver. ''You got to go home, Florice,'' she said, ''now.''

1943

He was standing in the shadows on Gorrell St. He had been there for two hours thinking she might be walking home from wherever she was. His hat was pulled down against the November wind. It was an old brown felt he had taken off someone after a fight on the job. Tobacco stained his teeth and his clothes, which smelled of the last work he had done in the tobacco packing house. He was making a little money now in Winston-Salem at the Brown Star tobacco warehouse. His match flared in the wind. It was getting dark. The bitch was probably somewhere playing good. Always playing good in some church. Damn wind had blown out his match. He struck another one, and was grabbed in the chest with a wheezing cough. He dropped the second match, but held on to the cigarette, scrounging in his pocket for another book of matches. The smoke filled his aching lungs. She had sure put his fire out. He hadn't really thought of her for years. Just coming through this town reminded him she was here. Wonder what she looked like now? She'd have a man all right, even as old as she was. There was no question about that. She was always hot. He knew she was always hot and she thought she was foolin' somebody with that stuff about God. He'd have to think about going soon. He needed another drink and tomorrow was his last day at the warehouse. He had to be there to pick up his check and move on. He smoked in the shadow of a large tree in the backyard. It seemed safe there. Nobody around. Folks all stuffin' themselves with Thanksgiving he reckoned. His old car stood on the street, about a block away, under the college dining room. Somebody said she worked there. Miss Smart Pants had found herself a job at a college!

She always did think she was better'n most folks. It was now full night. He could not be seen as he approached the kitchen window and looked into Rebecca's house. It was orderly and things were put away. There was a small light on over the sink. He stepped into the herb garden under the window, pressing large footprints onto the winter herbs that were left. He turned and saw a storage room to the left of the window. The outside door was slightly ajar.

He was walking a tight line. On one side was his sense of survival and pleasure which is all that kept him alive. And on the other side was the oily spill of bitterness that he occasionally slipped into and used to justify his cruelty which had become habitual with age.

He didn't know where the idea came from. It appeared like he did, on a dark street while the world was safe and comfortable behind lighted windows with full stomachs and warm fireplaces. It appeared and was mature all at once. He struck another match. She had to keep something out here like that, for storm lamps. It was on the top shelf. The third match went out. He threw it down and poured the kerosene over an old tablecloth she had stored there, and onto the floor.

They'd never find him. She hadn't heard tell of him since 1915 and he was traveling light now leaving no tracks behind. She oughta know. He wanted her to know she didn't kill him. He oughta leave a signature. He took out his pocket knife. There wouldn't be another soul who'd know about the pocket knife from a New Orleans shop. They had bought it together when they were young and silly, and he had used it to cut a hole for her in a stupid bird house. He knew she would remember that day. She was hot all right. She'd remember. Damn, he hadn't thought of her long legs for years. He stuck the knife in the tree he had been standing under so the pearl handle showed. So she'd remember. Struck the last match, threw it in the fire, and set out walking toward his car. His chest hurt like hell. Ardella's. When he got back to Winston he'd go back to Ardella's for a drink. She didn't have no nice tits, but she'd give a man a drink.

"But why now?" There seemed to be no rhyme or reason

to it. ''Why would he come back now?'' Florice was shaken. She had told only Alice about the knife. It wasn't found in all the excitement of the fire, and she didn't see it until Friday afternoon. Thank God for President Benedict. He had seen the fire from his front porch and called the fire department. The kitchen was ruined, but that had been thought a minor damage because all her personal things were saved, and the house was otherwise unharmed.

Alice threatened to tell the police herself. ''He subject to come back and get chu, gurl! It's just no question about it, you best tell the police he done done it! If I ever see the nigger, I gon kill him mahself!'' Florice told her to just hush up. Just hush up. She was not going to kill anybody at any time. ''You mindin' yo' own business, and he comin' like a thief in the night and you don't be lookin' for no trouble wid him all this twenty-eight years; *he* done run off, he done the runnin' off!''

''Alice, that's enough!'' she slammed the knife down on the sofa in Alice's living room. ''I got *my reasons*. And they ain't easy reasons. Now hush a minute.'' It was Friday night. They talked until 1:00 in the morning. How long does it take to tell a friend that the last time you saw your husband, so very long ago in another world, there were knives of pain in his eyes that you put there?

He had only stabbed the tree. She had betrayed. He had only been himself. She had declared a love for God, but her love for Theodore had been real and Mac saw it. He had known her at least that well. He had known she put her passion in the man, even if he would never have understood that it was the path God had chosen for her to walk toward herself. She knew that now. Theodore had God, and that was what she wanted, and so he was irresistible to her; but was it out of love or out of her own stubborn selfishness that she had betrayed? Theodore had shown her how to love the air and the rain and other people; he touched God's mysteries every day and he brought her to them. And so she did love him, and that was a betrayal to the young man with the knife, even though she never meant it to be so.

There is a price for betrayal. You collect the silver and

then you pay for it, again and again. Florice sighed. Would she ever finish paying? In the Bible there were only thirty pieces. She thought, we must all have silver hidden away in pouches, pieces and pieces, in the shadows, under beds, and behind our furnaces, old debts to be paid, betrayals to be tallied up, collected when we least expect it. No, she would never tell the police that she knew who set the fire.

At 7:00 that morning, Alice said, "Dey clean. You gon call?" "Of course," they said, "Ma'am," they said (because she was with the college), "we don't think we can find 'em. You realize you wiped away the prints. Don't ever touch the evidence. But we'll make a note of it, and we'll let you know."

"Yes, I'd like to know," she said. "I'd like to know if you catch him." But what she really wanted to say was, I'd like to know if he's still alive; if he's still a person; if I left him anything to live for; if he's ever been happy; if I just think I remember the knife and the young man I thought I loved and the passion of that day when he thought he loved me. I would like to know if I still owe for the silver.

1944

There was no way they could get her to go quietly. She was bitterly difficult, insisting that hospitals only cut you up when you don't need to be cut.

They had been arguing that day about something that didn't matter now. Something that had seemed important to them, and after all the words had been spoken, Alice had turned to her and said, "You best be rememberin', gurl, that life is like a dry tree. You can't lean on it."

Suddenly she had held on to her blouse under her breasts, and closed her eyes. Her skin was dark gray with pain.

Mr. Newell drove them to Brewer Memorial Hospital, Alice grimacing and silent, Florice shocked and angry that Alice had been so private about her sickness, remembering the life's blood that Alice had given her four years ago. The doctor was adamant about hospitalization. A perforated ulcer would mean death. It was clear she had been seeing the doctor for a long time, but had missed several appointments. They signed her in with difficulty, because she refused to answer the nurses' questions, so what Florice didn't know about her background, they left blank.

It was the night they usually sat up and planned the month's menus for the dining room. As awful as the physical pain was to Alice, it wasn't more intense than Florice's pain at the torn place between them. What had happened to make Alice think she couldn't tell her about the illness? She tried to concentrate on ordering her supplies, missing Alice so much she wiped tears from her menu cards.

It was like being lost in the desert, being separate and separated from Alice. She got up from her table to get a drink of water. And there was no way to heal the breach, no way to find out what was wrong. Alice was closed on the subject and, besides, you can't argue with a sick person. She felt no better after draining the glass. And there was no way to quench her thirst. She sat down again, determined to finish her work. Time seemed to push itself along like mud through a funnel. She got up again, looking for something to do. They had loved each other since 1916, since they were young and scared and ignorant of life. How could she do this? How could she just wipe it all off like she was cleanin' the kitchen table? And what if she should die in there? What if she should die and leave the dryness blowin' around her, leave her in this dust storm to get to the next oasis alone? Florice gave up, ordered the same supplies she had ordered last month, and went to bed, afloat on a sea of dust.

She was blessed with Harriet's friendship. They went to the hospital every afternoon, both of them quiet and worried. Harriet watching Florice carefully, Florice watching herself in order to stay in control.

Late that week as they walked into the ward, her heart seemed to fall forward into her chest. There was part of her that agreed with Alice. The hospital would probably do no good. She had no inner feeling that Alice was ever going to get well. Still, she didn't feel certain she wasn't either, and this was probably not the time to give up, she thought, looking at the tubes in Alice's arm. Harriet fussed and busied herself with pillows and curtains, calling nurses for this and that.

Alice looked at her dearest friend. "Don't fret yourself," she said. "The ole gurl got to give out once in a while. Don't fret yourself. I be comin' home soon's these doctors stop messin' with me. Be comin' home."

Florice shook her head. "We got to pray you well, Alice." They were touching. The landscape was familiar again.

Alice rose up as much as her strength would allow. "Rebecca Florice, I said, don't fret yourself. Now you *know* what I be sayin'. You hear me good. Don't chu fret yourself 'bout me." She fell back, exhausted. Harriet went looking for a nurse and pain pills. "Don't chu 'member what I tole you?

You can't lean on it," Alice said, her voice hushed but intense.

Then it was clear. Alice was refusing. Now she remembered the argument they had had a long week ago. It was about healing. It was about if you would know when your time came and what to do about it. Florice had said we should always try to help, and Alice had gotten angry and insisted that there was a time to leave things alone. She looked out at the street below, seeing but not seeing the doctors and patients come and go. Seeing the beginning of another ending. Alice was refusing.

She would pray. She would ask, for guidance, for wisdom, to know what to do, to know what to do. She prayed for hours. She was guided to try to heal, and then she was guided not to. After a while she couldn't tell the difference between her fear and her prayers and everything became a confusing mess of words and dread. And how she strained for the answers. How she tried. It made no sense to her. To be denied this one. This beloved one.

So Alice came home. And they welcomed her and she was happy, and for a while without pain, and for a while, it seemed as if things were back to normal. As long as Florice had known her, Alice had been stubborn about doctors and now she was stubborn about the diet, insisting that a diet for a baby was not gonna do a ole woman like her no good. Alice knew Florice had hope because she wanted to have hope, and in spite of what she really knew, anyhow, Alice thought to herself, Ain't nobody supposed to know everything. And she gave thanks for small mercies.

1945

She always wore two skirts, a shorter one on top, and a black one underneath that stayed dirty because of all the dust she raised with her broom. Some of the church deacons wondered if she should be put away, talking heathen the way she did about evil spirits. Fannie Lou cleaned and walked, walked and swept, sweeping out the corners of her porch steps all morning. Children on their way to school crossed the street and whispered about her terrible odor. She wore a cloth bag about the size of a walnut around her neck that stank of asphidity and garlic.

Far as she knew, there was still evil everywhere in spite of the good church deacons. Florice could see her black stockings rolled down to her ankles and the long gray underwear that showed beneath the skirts.

"Mornin', Miz Fannie Lou."

"Go 'head, go 'head, don't go back just go 'head." She took four steps forward and two back on "don't go back," and then one forward again on "go 'head." Florice knew she had been heard, but you didn't ever interrupt Miz Fannie Lou.

"Go 'head you ain't. Tell ole Pud, that somewheres else there's a home. You go 'head." She began to sweep again. "Go 'head you ain't. I said, tell old Pud . . ." Her voice trailed off in the sweeping dust. Fannie Lou's had a whole lot of sense in her time, Florice thought. She reached Alice's house about 10:00 and found her on the kitchen floor. She had died with her hands gripping her stomach.

Florice was on her knees. Her hands were in Alice's tangled hair. "Alice," she whispered, "Alice, tell ole Pud that somewhere's else there's a home. Tell old Pud, Alice, that somewhere's else there's a home."

1945

It was awful late. She could tell by the quiet. Sometimes she'd wake up like this. It was important to make sure nobody would get in cause Daddy was over there, long ways away, fightin' for them. She got up to get her stick. Used to belong to her own grandpa, Mama said. It was in the corner over by the door. The cat was lyin' on the sofa but she was not asleep. Ronnie could see her yellow eyes; they reflected the street lamp that showed through the living room curtains and made very mysterious shadows across the throw rug. Throw rug. What-not table. Dustin' the what-not table was her Saturday job. There was nobody there but she was real sure she had felt or heard something. Sometimes she'd feel things and people who wouldn't be there when she looked hard. Cat, go away. This was her job. Not your job, Cat.

And one day after Miss Alice died, she had talked to her. Mama was at Miss Florice's house, and she was there with her, and she went in the living room to look at the pretty soft rose-colored chair she liked to sit in with her legs crossed, and there she was, standin' over by the windows. She was sure it was Miss Alice 'cause she had on a blue dress that was her favorite and she couldn't see her face good, but it was her, she was sure and she said, "How you, Ronnie?" and she said, "Fine, how you, Miss Alice," and then Miss Florice said from the kitchen, "Ronnie, who you talkin' to?" And Miss Alice had vanished just like that.

Something. Take her stick and look in the kitchen. Not to wake Mama. She be mad. Something. And her job to see everything be safe. Then it rang. The doorbell really did ring. And Mama turned on a light, blinkin', and said, "Ron-

nie? What in the world?'' and said, ''Who is it?'' soundin'
all worried, and said ''Just a minute,'' and ''What?'' and
said, ''Oh my God, my God'' and she couldn't open the door
good cause she was laughin' and cryin' and then this man
who was pickin' her up and kissin' and kissin' and huggin'
and huggin', and ''That's my daddy home,'' and ''That's my
daddy home from the war!''

1946

It was like sinking in quicksand, except you knew there was a bottom. Running on the crunchy surface held a delicious fear and certain knowledge that sooner or later the crust would break and the snow would swallow you up to your waist. She would stay out as long as they'd let her, so cold it was, so new. It had not snowed like this in North Carolina since Ronnie's birth. Her nose hurt and her toes felt funny. The dog sounded so far away when he was right there, but the snow made an echo of everybody's voice. She bounced on it to see how long it would hold her weight and crashed through just for the love of crashing. There was power in knowing exactly what would happen but not knowing when.

She wondered, What would they do to her if she just didn't come in? What if she just walked and walked or hid out in the old shack at the end of the street until they were all excited? What would they do to find her? Would they call the police or something terrible like that? She shook the snow off her gloves. It was not good to get too much snow on your gloves, 'cause they would turn wet and your fingers would hurt.

By this time Ronnie was at the end of the block. The abandoned shed was right around the corner. She'd always wanted to see inside it. In the distance, she could hear the voices of the other children, high voices bouncing off the snow they so seldom saw. It was the purple time of day and somebody's mother cut through the haze yelling, "Waldene, you come in this minute, 'fore I beat yo' ass!" Only it was all so foggy to Ronnie, like a dream remembered, and where she was was the only reality. She turned the corner and stepped into the backyard which surrounded the shed. There was a fence she had to climb, but it was rickety and not very high, and there was a place where she could just step through. Slowly, watching her footprints in the snow, she approached the door; it had been recently cracked, and snow blew in through the crack. Her eyes adjusted to the dark. It seemed safe enough. She opened the door and stepped through. Old tires. Faint smell of oil and rubber. An ancient pair of huge coveralls in a heap on the ground. Odor of lingering garbage, and something else she couldn't name. Apple core and an empty beer can; the label still said *Lucky Pintos*. Two liquor bottles. There were pictures of four red roses on each one. Ronnie didn't understand what red roses had to do with that stuff men drank. Funny thing to put on the bottle, she thought. Her rubber boots made the only sound she could hear. On the left side of the shed. Under the little window. Faint purple light filtered by dust, and a rag wound around something. Ronnie found a stick so she could poke. Something there. She couldn't get it undone with that stick. She got down on her knees. Someone had tied it tight. There. There was a rotten place in the rag. It fell apart in two pieces. Ronnie's hand froze around the end of her short stick. She backed off, crawling backwards, banging the Four Roses bottles together. In the science book at school. In the science book. She had seen that. She knew what that was. Bones. Bones looked just like that. It had to be a hand.

She threw up on the snow just before the hole in the fence. Get home. Get home was all she could hear herself saying. Several houses down the street in the purple twilight, Peaches paused to make sure she had her night's bottle in her pocket.

* * *

They had been kneeling behind the sofa for about thirty minutes. Trudy lived a few houses down the street and her mama was almost never home. She spent the night with Ronnie at least twice a week. The girls never talked about Trudy's mama, but Ronnie had always thought Trudy was a liar. She would say things, things like: "We have a radio, too. Only ours is bigger than yours. Mama listens to her stories and irons.'' Things like: ''Mama be real busy goin' shoppin' for us,'' or ''Why don't y'all get one of them new Kalvinators? Mama say she gonna get us one real soon.''

Ronnie was trying hard to hear what Miss Florice was saying about somebody's ''hard won happiness'' when Trudy said ''Girl, yo' legs sho is ashy. Don't you know to put on some Blue Seal? Mama say Vaseline is the thang to keep yoself well oiled.'' Ronnie said nothing about how much Trudy needed to comb her hair. Her knees were sore. She motioned for Trudy to be quiet. She made her sick sometimes. ''Hush, girl,'' Ronnie said, ''You wanna get caught?''

Their voices always tasted like peppermint to Ronnie as they talked delicious adult talk on a summer evening. Mama and Miss Florice, on the front porch starin' into the dark. Screens made it easy to hear. Or would have, except that Trudy was such a nuisance.

''You know she has TB.'' They muffled the last word as if the porch itself contained some white-shirted authority that would punish them just for saying ''TB.'' Ronnie knew all about the fourteen bottles of cheap wine that had been found under Sara Helkin's bed when she died and about the fat man she kept company with from Atlanta, and she knew that Aunt Doris Fannis really hated her husband but was afraid to leave him. Leave him to go where? Did anybody ever leave a husband? Miss Florice's husband had left her and was never heard of again, except she had heard Miss Alice fussin' once about that son of somethin'. Ronnie thought of Mama leaving Daddy or Daddy leaving Mama—would be like the grass leaving the ground. Ronnie wondered about Miss Florice. She had never had a husband long as she could remember. Even when she was real little. Ronnie had always wondered why she didn't get married again and nobody ever talked about it. It was like TB she guessed . . . you weren't supposed to talk about it.

''I'm tired being down here, com'on. Le's go play with the sewin' kit.''

''She could have, Florice,'' Mama was sayin. ''She really could have. Who knows for sure? You don't know what people might do.'' Miss Florice said something she could barely hear about "evidence" and "never finding the . . ." something and her voice faded.

"They said it was *no hand* on the body when they found it," said Mama. "Gives me the creeps just to think of *that*. Downright ungodly. Lord. Why are we talkin' about that old stuff anyway, Florice, it happened years ago. Ronnie was just a baby. Lord, time flies." The porch swing creaked once or twice. Ronnie had forgotten about Trudy after she heard the word "hand." Nobody knew about that. She hadn't told *nobody*. Oh Lordy suppose there was somethin' to what she had seen? Maybe she should tell somebody and then what? She'd be in big trouble for goin' in that shed and maybe bigger trouble even. A body? Oh Lordy.

"Ronnie!" Trudy whispered loud enough to let anybody know where they were hiding. "I *said*, let's go! I'm tired bein' down here!" Ronnie jumped back to the present and dropped her jackrocks with a terrifying clatter.

"Girls?" It was Mama. She called in through the open window. Ronnie's heart was beating hard, but the ladies didn't move. "Time for bed. Put your toys up now and go wash up." The swing squeaked another one or two times.

She had run up on the front porch that evening like something was after her, and Mama was standing there looking out over the snow, worried to death and there wasn't anything she could say 'cause she was gettin' scolded at for being out in the snow till "nearly dark, nearly dark" and Mama pullin' at her snow boots and takin' off the wet things as fast as she could lecture about catchin' her death of cold and so on. And she had to take a hot bath and eat some soup and go to bed. So she just never was asked where she had been, and that was fine with Ronnie cause she wasn't tellin' anyhow. She had dreams about hands for a long time, but she wasn't tellin'. When Miss Florice and Mama started talkin' about a hand that summer, she remembered she hadn't told, and her worries started and her dream so she couldn't stand it, and she thought maybe she should tell Miss Florice 'cause Mama would kill her for goin' in that place.

Mama was at the doctor's. Ronnie was watching Miss Florice weed flowers and being told which were weeds and which were flowers. "Now that's nasturtium," she was saying to Ronnie. "Can you say that? And that's marigold and snapdragon's next to that. Don't pull up anything that looks like that."

Suddenly Ronnie said, "I saw it." She let out a nervous sigh. Miss Florice thought she would put in another bed next year. Snapdragons were getting thin. "What say, Ronnie?" She peered at the child from under her straw hat.

"I saw it, Miss Florice."

"Saw what, honey?" She was listening carefully now. Ronnie bit her lower lip. She dug her toe into the nasturtium bed. "That thing. Those bones." "What bones?" Florice was very still. Ronnie had been so old for so long. Florice wiped her forehead and fanned with her hat.

"Over there in the shed, you know, around the corner from our house. I saw bones and bottles with four roses on 'em, and a pair of old dirty coveralls."

Florice said, carefully, "Maybe you just thought they were bones, baby. You know sometimes we think we see things. We just *think* we do. Coulda been some old dog's bones." But she knew. Already the child could see far more than she could. Ronnie looked stubborn and determined. Florice could tell, there was no going back here.

"I saw 'em," Ronnie said, "and they looked like that picture in the science book at school of what bones are inside your hands." Then Florice knew. She knew who did it, and she knew she knew. There would be no more putting off the decision.

"Well, now, you just let me worry about that, sugar. Don't you worry your head one more minute, you hear? Whatever you saw it's not your fault you saw it. And nothin's gonna happen to you. So don't you worry."

"You and Mama. I heard you and Mama talkin' one night 'bout a hand or somethin', and a body."

Florice tightened her lips. "Ain't nothin' concernin' you. You just get that outa your mind and if you see anything else, tell me. Now let's get us some lunch. Gettin' hot out here."

1946

She had been in the backyards of all of them like a giant squid thrown up on the beach, half awake, considered harmless for the most part. And now Florice would have to deal with this nightmare that stayed balanced on the edge of sanity only because it took tea in her parlor. Peaches, in jail. Peaches in a mental hospital; or dead. Peaches who had lived and worked and blessed them all with her gelatinous presence, was now a monster who must be reckoned with. She had shown up every week for five years on Florice's front porch because that was the only place in the world she had ever felt full. She had started combing her hair, and now washed her overalls once in a while. Florice sat down by her bedroom window and Robert flashed through her mind. God gives gifts, she thought, and they are much to be feared. The more wonderful they are, the more they hurt. In captivity Peaches would become the demon Florice had held at bay and put to sleep. Or they would shock her senseless, or they would kill her. Florice had a vision of Peaches, a mountain of fat cells, confused, terrified, and somewhere inside, a soul in unbearable pain. She fingered the china box from Robert. It held her most prized jewelry including the cross Theodore had given her. And they would strap her down and make her scream in pain and for what?

She had a habit of asking Florice for food scraps for her dog, a dog she had found down near her shack. He was a starving, dying, stray. She combed him every day. Brushed and combed, combed and brushed, flourishing all the care on him she had never had, and he got well. She had named him Louis, for Joe Louis. He did what her whiskey and food

124

could not do. Her whiskey was an angry enemy she couldn't do without. Her food wasn't loved, it was just stuffed; like stuffing a mattress over and over. But Louis, Louis would follow her to the bus, wait at the bus stop while she was working, and follow the bus back to the colored side of town. Peaches told Florice Louis knew he was colored 'cause he never went to the white lady's house with her, just to the bus stop. She fed him before she fed herself.

What if she didn't do it? What if she kept silent? Those others who didn't know Peaches was a demon sleeping, they would be at the mercy of a monster who swam in and out of their lives, and she would become a shield for Peaches until she decided to kill again. She closed her eyes, feeling the burden of the mystery once more. If you could just know, if you could just be sure of anything, just for a little while. Alice was gone and Harriet would just call the police with no hesitation. Murder was murder, she would say. She sat for two, maybe three hours, doing needlework, looking at the street below, listening, praying, being alone with the thing. The sun was going down and she heard the thrush who lived in the wooded field next door, and the bobwhite and the voice of a child somewhere. It came on slowly. She would get there, to that place where she was lowered gently into space, floating, needing not to notice her own heartbeat, her own presence in this world. The rocking chair was almost still. In this nether space she saw a ball of underwater emerald green slowly form. It floated toward her gently and settled in her lap. Her hands were still and rested on the arms of the chair. They became violet and green, white in turn and finally a core of violet covered her from head to toe. She was closed in deep stillness as the light played her body and she began to pivot and turn in the circle of light until the white blinded her and she was truly no longer Florice, but only dimly conscious of being at all. After a while, the turning slowed and stopped and the colors faded and went out. Something was pulling at her mind to come back to the rocking chair, to the window, to Florice. She opened her eyes reluctantly, stubbornly, as if to do so would be to violate something sacred. Her hands were in her lap. The room was dark. Joe Louis would have to do it.

She was mopping the front porch when it was time for Peaches' next visit. There was a bucket of soapy water on the steps and a broom was up against the house near the door. Florice saw them coming and took a deep breath. Harriet and Ronnie would stay home today, Ronnie had a cold. Peaches walked up and sat on the steps without a word. Joe Louis trotted patiently behind her. He was a brown and black shorthaired mongrel. Somebody had cut his tail once.

"Nice day, ain't it?" Peaches said.

Florice answered quietly, "Yes it is." She wrung out the mop and went over the porch once more. As she finished, Peaches started up the steps and so did Louis. He always waited for her right outside the front door. Suddenly Florice turned, grabbed the broom and flew at Louis, knocking him sideways and off the porch. He yelped and howled and scattered off, a surprised and hurt sound in the distance, and Florice turned around, facing Peaches and said, "Don't bring that dog on my clean porch with his feet muddy ever again!"

Peaches began to flush from her large neck upward. She reached inside her overalls for her liquor bottle and broke it on the door frame. The smell of whiskey rushed out, covering the soap odor, and the liquid splashed all over the immaculate porch. The big woman clenched her free hand. Rebecca Florice whose full height was 5'5" would have appeared frail if there had been any witnesses. She watched Peaches carefully, all her senses alive. Perhaps Peaches thought that after all there was no real contest here; perhaps she was saving her real response for later. Not really understanding, herself, what made her stop the broken bottle in midair, but feeling the deep confusion of having a friend suddenly turn, Peaches dropped her hands, and the liquor bottle. She turned and left the house, lumbering awkwardly in her hurry to be away from this awful conflict, the first time she could ever remember not wishing death to an "enemy," and entirely undone at this change in herself.

After Florice's attack, Louis had run off and had not come back. Peaches went down to the old shack two days after the porch scene. She could see her package had been tampered with. Somebody had been there. Grief for the missing Joe Louis kept her mind off who might have seen the bones. She wrapped her package back up. "That old white bitch," she mumbled, "who cares if I did kill her?" Anyhow, she deserved it. The bitch had slapped her face. Didn't nobody slap Peaches and get away with it. "Don't take no shit from nobody," she said aloud. "And don't nobody hit my dog either, not nobody." She tried several times to get up, steadying herself against the wall. "I'll just go kick ass; uppity woman. Always was uppity and strange. Didn't never have no man. Folks used to say she was 'tetched, mentally minded.' " She laughed. The shack door creaked open and she tried to remember the way to Florice's house. "My dog's gone," she said to nobody. "My dog's gone, and I ain't right without my dog, and she did it, my only frien', my only frien'. . . ."

She used her fist for a door knocker. The sound of her screen door bouncing with each blow startled Florice who was just closing windows on her way to bed. Startled, but not surprised; she had expected her before now. She bowed her head and opened the door. Peaches was dressed in a discarded oversized raincoat which reached to ten inches below her knee, and a pair of men's trail shoes. Florice could tell she was very drunk.

"Peaches, what you doing here this time of night?" Florice asked in her most concerned voice. "You, you done run him away. You done it." "Come on in now, Peaches, let's have some coffee and talk." She guided her through the living room. Peaches looked puzzled. She had almost forgotten what she had come here to do. This woman was her friend. The one who had told her she was a person, a real person, and she liked this place and this friend. She stepped into the kitchen and Florice put a tentative hand on her fleshy shoulder. Peaches shook her off, made her way into the kitchen and set heavily in a chair. They looked at each other. "Where my dog, Miss Florice? Where my dog?" She was clearly threatening. Rebecca Florice knew it was this night she had to make up her mind. "I don't know, Peaches. Reckon he went away to change his life a little, reckon he was mad at me for beatin' his tail.''

"Wouldn'ta done it, 'cept'n, 'cept'n you hit him,'' she heard Peaches say, almost to herself.

"I'm real sorry about that, Peaches. You know I am. I guess I was just fussy and mean that day and I had just got beside myself. You know how your nerves can get. I was really hoping you'd forgive me.'' She had been looking at Peaches, who was looking at her own left hand and who slowly began to close her hand into a fist and then open it, close it and then open it. Her forearm was as big as two of Florice's. Florice kept hearing an old gospel song go through her head as she watched Peaches carefully. "I know it was the blood, I know it was the blood, I know it was the blood for me.'' That song kept singing inside her. If it was to be, it was to be.

Peaches pounded on the table once, then twice. She hadn't touched her coffee, but the liquor was beginning to wear off. "Don't let nobody give me no shit,'' she mumbled. Her eyes looked into the corner of the kitchen where the broom was leaning against the wall.

"Joe Louis was mine. He was mine.'' She hit the table three times. The cups shook and the salt shaker turned over. Florice looked at it, but she sat very still, sipping her coffee. In that five minutes she thought of Harriet and of Ronnie and of all of them who didn't know that there was, indeed, a murderer walking among them, and of poor Peaches whose one link with human compassion had been taken from her, and who had been and would be, so tortured and so agonized, and who might have to die just because she was a victim of a loveless spiral that had no beginning. "I know it was the blood,'' her mind sang. "I know it was the blood.''

Florice had been saving a special jar of pickles to give Harriet's husband for his birthday. It dropped into her mind all at once. She got up quietly and reached for it in the lower cupboard.

Pleading silently for both their lives, she slid the jar across the table at Peaches, who had been looking around the kitchen very carefully. The jar was wrapped in white tissue paper with a small ribbon. "For you. I'm truly sorry about the dog, Peaches. I beg your pardon." The tears in the great puffy face began to water. She was crying for Louis, but she was crying for herself most of all. For all the old gone days when she was a child alone and ugly, a little fat girl whose father always stank of alcohol and whose mother was in a stunned absent silence all the time. Whose home was a small trailer of three rooms and whose only friend had left her because she said her mama said she couldn't play with a girl whose mama was a nigger and whose daddy was white trash. There had been a dog then, a dog her daddy took out to look for coon, and he used to be tied up in the back and howl all night. He licked his water from a dirty old tin can that had mud in it. One day she was changing the water, and her daddy had slapped her across the face and said to leave the dog alone, cause it was his dog and he didn't want him eatin' outa nobody else's hand, and she had cried a long time 'cause her face hurt her so, and the dog had to drink that dirty water. And then one day he died and she had found him when she was out hangin' up clothes on the fence. The dog was dead, and she knew her daddy was gonna blame her. She hadn't done nothin', but he was gonna blame her 'cause he always did. So she buried him. She dragged him off and buried him way down by the dump and she lied and said he run away. He just run away. And he beat her anyway 'cause he said she had untied him and it was her fault he didn't have no huntin' dog.

She cried for herself, for the little girl who was always hungry, and because nobody had ever given her a present before. She was clutching the jar of pickles. "Maybe he be back, Miss Florice, you reckon?" And she got up to go, rubbing the jar on the table. The label read: "Florence Letenielle, 1946 Bread and Butter Pickles."

"Maybe so, Peaches," said Florice smiling.

"I sho do 'ppreciate this here present. You's a good woman, Miss Florice. I hears what you say 'bout treatin' folks nice. I just never had nothing 'fore Joe Louis. Never before. Well, I'm back like before." She shook her head and blew her nose on a napkin, "It ain't just me and my dog, it's just me. But I tell you what, Miss Florice, I'm gonna keep this jar forever 'cause you give it to me and that say somethin', don't it? That say somethin'.''

Florice would watch her for many days after that. She would watch her watching the children from the corner. She would notice the set of the jaws, the eyes that met hers when Peaches would come over for her weekly visit. One day when Joe Louis returned as mysteriously as he had left, Florice decided that it was time to get rid of the bones altogether. Peaches had long forgotten her drunken evening when she had last noticed the pile of bones.

Florice waited until one day when she knew Peaches would be at work. She took a small garden scoop, and a brown paper sack. It was just daybreak. The fact of what she was doing, she had to put on a shelf in her mind. There was no other way to do it. Half looking at the small pile of bones, she quickly scooped them up into her bag, and carefully left everything else as she had found it. Only the milkman was up. Florice waited by the fence until he had done the street, and walked home, avoiding Harriet's house by going out of the way. No one would ever have to carry this burden but her. There were some things to keep between you and God. (And maybe Alice, she thought, who was somewhere shaking her head and saying, "Lord, gurl. Lord, Lord, what chu gon do next?")

1947

Light comes in cracks. Somebody peeing. She heard the water and knew it was Daddy. Too much water for anybody else. Faint light through her door on the orange crates Mama had used for night tables. This was the day they were going to the flea market. Ronnie would never forget the light on the crates, and the morning pee. The special day. They were to begin very early, take the bus to Madison, and spend the day looking for things they needed. She felt the ice-wood floor on her bare feet, tumbling out of bed to hurry for this exciting trip, out of town. Out of town always had that exciting sound to it like when white folks said, "abroad"—"She went abroad." Ronnie wasn't sure what abroad was but it sounded wonderful. Well, she wasn't going there, she was going "out of town" and it was just as good. She hadn't turned on the light because Mama would be sure to say it was still too early. But she could hear them, Mama and Daddy, getting him out for work. The sounds she would remember for a lifetime, muffled loves of moving routine, to bring in the greens and the beans to keep them alive. Somehow she knew, even at eight, that Daddy's early rising was hard put and wrung out of a need for them not to want for anything. "Y'all won't want for anything if I can help it," he would say, "long as I'm breathin'," he said, and she would always feel her insides turn with a fear that he might not always be breathin', and she and Mama would be alone, really alone. Often she saw the glint of hatred in his eyes when he said that.

Light comes through cracks. The floor was really cold and the coffee smell meant that they were settled at the kitchen table. Ronnie remembered there would be fried chicken for lunch when she heard Mama take out the big iron skillet. She slid under the covers for another warm hour, convinced that they were really going, out of town.

Why did they call it that? The flea market. Pictures in her mind of fleas in little cages for sale, different prices for big ones, little ones, small bunches, large bunches. Miss Florice said maybe they called it that because when you got so much junk together, fleas and all manner of crawling things collected. There sure was enough junk at this flea market. It was a big field and there were tables and tables of junk and miles and miles of people wandering around. Ronnie saw everything she could imagine people could use or want in this world! Stuff rich white folks had bought and thrown away. Mama said they didn't need it in the first place. Miss Florice said, "Didn't need it, didn't want it, and couldn't use it. It was mostly too ugly to have in the house, would scare you to come in the house at night with that stuff peering out of the corners." There was even a bed with black posts, big round black balls on the posts, a big chest of drawers with ugly white knobs, and a mirror with curly-cues all around it.

Somebody had a pet monkey that kept jabberin', and Mama said, "Anything that smelled like that ought to have been kept in Africa in the first place, but then there's no accountin for what white folks'll do." She thought those chickens Mama kept smelled almost as bad but she didn't say so. Never seen so much glass and junk. "Antiques" was what the sign said, and the glass was different colors in the rainbow. The clean pieces glittered in the sun, but it was awful expensive, she thought.

Miss Florice found her a nice box to keep stuff in, and some big pots for cookin' a mess of greens and pintos and things. Harriet got a lamp and a small rug. She was all the time cluckin' her tongue about how folks could throw out perfectly good things and on and on.

Twenty-five cents. She had a fortune. Some time to look and spend it in. Also a fortune. Ronnie sauntered. She sauntered, for this was savoring time. She was really twenty years old, looking for furniture for her house. She was about to "set up housekeeping" as the grown folks always called it. That sounded so important. *Set up* housekeeping. That chest was too tall, this one too dark. It took a long time that twenty-five cents. It took her to China with cast-off lacquered slippers that smelled of incense and Chicago's Chinatown, it took her to a rich evening with oil lamps and crystal chandeliers, and to the fearful and mysterious time called slavery—to runaway posters with faces of her own people, worth one and two thousand dollars. "Only a quarter." The old woman peered down at her through those thick glasses that made your eyes look like a dot at the bottom of a whirlwind. Gave Ronnie chills to look at her. Slapped down the quarter, grabbed the wanted poster and ran. Suddenly she desperately needed the presence of Mama and Miss Florice. They couldn't do that anymore, could they? Sell you for a thousand dollars? What could she really see through those circles?

Lunch was at the bus stop in Madison. No colored could go in the park or restaurants, and Mama said 'fore she'd eat in the kitchen, they'd put her underground. Miss Florice didn't say nothin' till later when she whispered to Mama, "They can kiss my Black ass." And Ronnie said to herself, "Right." So the bus stop it was, pleasant, free, and under the green trees. Miss Florice brought potato salad in little cups, and Mama had fried chicken, and Ronnie thought she'd bust wide open by the time the Greensboro bus drove up. That was when she almost lost it, all the chicken.

Ah, the hope in the heart—the natural, the human—that when one is weary one should be allowed, even expect, to sit down. Employers have it and yet deny it, mothers have it and yet deny it, husbands have it and yet deny it, and those who rule others have it and yet deny it. And so they boarded the bus, heavy with dearly bought treasures and full of human hope. COLORED TO THE REAR hung in resplendent red. The resplendent pink person spread himself over seats that at least one large and one small person could have used.

Rebecca Florice Letenielle always carried an umbrella. "It might rain," she would say, simply. It covered a multitude of explanations. On that day in that bus it rained. Mama with shopping bag, woman warrior with umbrella, and very small person saw the leg as it moved to a position of you-niggers-will-not-sit-next-to-me. Mama with shopping bags, and very small person, saw the woman warrior, the umbrella and the leg move all at the same time. In a blue blur, the weapon, the leg and the noise of synthetic leather impacted, and somewhere between swallowing her faint nausea of fear, and eternity, Ronnie heard Rebecca Florice Letenielle say to her, "Now you sit down." Scare had a strange power, fascination even. Ronnie knew she had seen her history. They could not sell her now, not even for five thousand dollars.

"Mama," she said, as they walked home from the bus stop in the mossy twilight, "kids at school say it's white folks all over the world. That so?"

"Yes, baby, sure is so for a fact. But you know what? One place they ain't. They ain't living and breathin' in your heart. You keep the Good Lord in your heart, you won't have to worry 'bout no white folks, and no seats on no bus. You still scared?" Ronnie was still clutching her wanted poster. "Mama, some day I'm gonna carry Miss Florice's umbrella for her. Don't it get heavy?"

* * *

"I oughta have my hair fixed, you know, honey? A woman can't look too good and you never know when somebody'll come along, I mean I'll get lucky soon, I can just feel it. Antoinette says if she was free, why there'd be just buckets of men callin' on her, but she's married, you know, I mean really married and anyhow she just got goo gobs of offers all the time and it pays to be ready, so I says to her, honey. . . ." Ronnie wandered off the sidewalk onto the grass, ahead of Mama and "Her Dizziness." Miss Florice had named her friend Selma, "Her Dizziness." She said dizzy meant silly and that meant Selma didn't know if her head was on straight.

Ronnie reminded herself that Selma had said "hair fixed" and not "head fixed," and began to play imaginary hopscotch on the sidewalk. It was beginning to rain. She wished they would walk faster because the tips of her toes were beginning to get cold, or *colder*, and the bus stop was not so close to their house. Selma would turn off soon unless she decided to come home with them, which Ronnie hoped she wouldn't because that meant Mama wouldn't be able to concentrate on dinner and wouldn't make something real good, but they'd have plain green beans and boiled potatoes or something like that and no dessert. Ronnie began to say to herself, "Turn off, Selma, turn off, Selma, turn off, Selma," like she did when she wanted it to snow—let it snow today, let it snow today.

Mama liked Selma, she thought, but Selma scattered her like a marble does when you shoot at a pile. And when Selma went home, Mama piled herself back up and was all together after a few minutes. Usually she'd say, "whew," and close the door with a push like when she was closin' a too full closet.

They neared Selma's street and Ronnie thought about dinner and listened for the good-byes, whispering, "Turn off, Selma, turn off, Selma," then she heard her mother say how chilly it was and she heard Selma say, "Well, sure, if you insist, honey, I could use a good cup of your coffee, you know, nobody can make it like you do, you know. I used to go with a man said that coffee was the reason many folks were still married 'cause it kept lots of wives outa men's hair, hee hee. . . ." and Ronnie gave up all hopes of dessert as she kicked the nearest pebble into the gutter and started down the front walk to their door.

"Guess who's at home?" She was fingering the home-made chocolate chip cookie Miss Florice had given her because it was always better to wait as long as possible and let the good seep in through your nose and up your fingers to your mouth. "Well, let me see now," said Florice, knowing, of course, who was at home and exactly why she found the eight-year-old at her tea table. "It could be the Petersons from church."

"No, not them, they only come on Saturday night to play checkers."

"Well, it could be Mr. Sampson, your dad's old friend from South Carolina."

"Nope, not him. I like him; he laughs a lot."

"Could be your Aunt Clara spendin' the weekend?"

"No, it isn't any of them, Miss Florice." Ronnie had taken that first careful bite of the warm cookie and there was a crumb falling off her chin which Florice firmly wiped with a napkin, between "Miss" and "Florice."

"Oh, and who is it then, Miss Ronalda Johnstone? Who could send you running over here for hot cookies and milk so close to dinnertime?"

"Well, who else?" Ronnie said in her most grown-up disgusted tone, "Her Dizziness."

"Well, chile, the Lord made all kinds of people, dizzy and otherwise. Some of us got talents we show, others got talents we give, and others got talents we don't know we got yet. Maybe she ain't heard hers yet."

"What you mean 'heard hers'?"

"Just that. You listen to yourself well enough and long enough and you'll hear what you do best. Now take you, for instance, you too little to hear so good. You got lots of time and work to do 'fore you can hear good."

"But 'Her Dizziness' is way old'n me, and I . . ."

"Wait a minute. Now you see, Ronnie, Selma might be a little deaf, because for one thing she talks so much she has turned off her inside ear."

"Inside ear?"

"Inside ear."

Ronnie chewed quietly and sipped milk quietly and waited for more. Part of her knew she would have to ask, part of her wanted Miss Florice just to give out the lesson without being asked, but she never did that. Ronnie finished a whole cookie. Finally she blurted out, "What's an inside ear?"

"Wondered when you'd ask," said Florice, squinting at the milk bottle. "Well, now, an inside ear is invisible, untouchable, and something lots of folks don't know they have. But that's the ear you hear with when all else fails. When somethin' tells us to stay in on certain days, 'cause, well, we don't know why, we just thought we'd better stay home, that's the ear we hear it with. And that's the ear we hear with when we know we was meant to do somethin' and that the Good Lord wants us to do it. And we'll hear all about ourselves if we learn to be quiet and listen. But poor Selma is about deaf, you see, as far as that ear is concerned. Her inside ear has almost died from lack of use, I 'speck. So really you should feel sorry for her, 'cause she got one less ear than you.''

Ronnie chewed the last chew and knew it was time to go. But she wanted to be dismissed, because she knew that she would be, and she liked the ritual.

''See the rainbow now?''

''Yes, ma'am.''

''As much as you can?''

''No, 'cause I ain't tall enough.''

''But you will be.''

''Yeah. Bye.''

''Bye. Hello to your mama.''

Once when she was little, really little, Ronnie could almost remember, there had been a summer shower while they were visiting Miss Florice. The shower was so brief, they sat it out on the front porch, Ronnie, her mama, and Florice. With the parting of clouds, there was a rainbow, the first in Ronnie's recollection and Florice held her up to see over the evergreens in the yard. Those words had been passed between them and never forgotten by either. Florice always knew what she was waiting for at the close of each visit, and she always gave what was needed.

1949

That day started with Mama's usual Saturday trip for groceries and Ronnie's usual job of breakfast dishes, and beds to be made, but it didn't end that way. Along about noon, Miss Florice rang the doorbell and opened the screen all at the same time. "Ronalda Jackson Johnstone, where you?" Ronnie knew it was play and not trouble even if Miss Florice was using her whole name 'cause this was her birthday and she knew it would be a good time ahead. "Yes, ma'am?" she answered smartly.

"You know you heard me ring that doorbell, girl, you ain't finished those dishes yet? We got a place or two to go, *this* birthday what's here!"

There was always a trip of some kind. Mama and Miss Florice would cook up something, and then Daddy would come home for ice cream and cake and there would be Chinese checkers and lemonade later on.

Today she was ten. A full decade. And Miss Florice said anyone who lived a decade deserved a special surprise. Mama came down from the attic wearing her spring hat for the occasion and told Ronnie to get on her Sunday shoes. She knew it was special then. Sunday shoes were never allowed in the midweek except for school programs, so it had to be special! They made a threesome, Miss Florice and her umbrella, Mama and her spring straw, and Ronnie in her black patent leather Sunday shoes. She could hardly stand not asking, but knew it was against the rules of the game, so she bit her lip, all the time trying to figure out where they were headed. As they neared downtown, she counted cracks in the sidewalk to keep from bustin' out, "Where're we going?"

They passed the colored library and the sweet shoppe, spelled "shoppe" and Ronnie thought for the thousandth time, Wonder why its called a shoppie? but she didn't even ask that. Finally they were there—at the corner of Elm and Washington and at the biggest department store in town. Ronnie held her breath as they went through the door. It smelled of powders, perfumes and richness and there was a kind of hum inside she always heard when there were lots of dressed up ladies together anywhere. She was very quiet. Mama had a little smile on her face, Miss Florice's eyes were secretive. The elevator made that queer jolt it had when it reached a floor and they got on, stepping to the rear, like the lady said. She didn't like being smashed into all those white bodies but the excitement was enough to make that a minor annoyance. They were going to the girls' department. The Girls' Department, with its striped candy canes and pink ruffles and blue and white artificial flowers and rows and rows of otherworld fairytale dresses! As she stepped off the elevator and into the wishworld of GIRLS 7–12 Ronnie guessed that they were going to buy her a dress, a store-bought party dress. It was too much for her. She swallowed her gum. Elmer said if you swallowed your gum all your insides would stick together, but what did boys know? What did boys know indeed on this wondrous day? There was blue and yellow to be chosen from, not just blue and yellow, but cloud blue and yellow from buttercups, there was red velvet and white lace collar, and green taffeta with tucks and, oh my, white organza! Mama said not over six dollars. She edged up to each one and glanced quickly at the price tag to see if she could risk liking it. Miss Florice was glaring at the clerk who did the usual clucking in the nice nasty tone of "Can I help you girls," which told them they were Black and therefore might steal or at the very least contaminate these dresses which were really made for little white girls in golden curls. Miss Florice held her at bay with her umbrella and Ronnie took her sweet time. "Finally!" Mama said as Ronnie triumphantly turned with "This one." Then there was the trying on. The turning, the twisting, the checking, and the nod they knew all the time she would give—even before she put it on.

The clerk stuffed it in the box, Miss Florice had insisted on a box with a flourish of her umbrella—and she stuffed it with an incredible urgency as if to get them out of there as fast as possible.

Ronnie worried about her blue satin sash all the way home. She held murder in her heart in reserve for the clerk. If there was any damage to her powder blue lace dress and her satin sash when she got home, she would return it to that store herself, and with a poison dart hide behind the nearest dummy and spit, hard.

The breath was held as they opened the box for Daddy. It was blue, it was lacy and it was not smashed. It was hers alone. Happy ten years, happy candles wrapped up in blue sashes, and ice cream dreams that night.

1950

"Florice, you know I heard from June just the other day. Sent me a postcard from some church conference up north, I think it was Pittsburgh or something." Florice was mildly interested in the choir member's chatter, thinking with part of her brain about something else while they waited for the bus to arrive. "Anyhow, she mentioned that she had seen Rev Brown, you know, *our* Rev Brown." Had the choir's staunchest member been really up to her standards, she would have noticed the grip tightened on Rebecca Florice's umbrella and the slight purse of the lips, but she didn't.

"Said Rev Brown wasn't doin' so good, was real thin. Had a operation last month, and has a temporary assignment in a small church up there. And Lord, Florice, his wife left him! Seems to me temporary assignments always means they don't really want you, you know what I mean? Well, is he standin' in for someone else or what? And imagine, left a big church like ours to *fill in* for someone? Well, the Lord sure surprised us on that one. I would have pegged him for a *big* success . . ."

The bus could have come and gone; Florice would not have seen it but for a voice somewhere that said—hold on till you get home. Don't let on what you're feelin'. Her stop finally came and she let her mouth tighten all the way home. Well, it really wasn't her fault. She tried to tell him, tried and tried . . . they should have been together, they should have been together and he wouldn't have been alone, and she wouldn't have been alone . . . she had always ended up that way, always, always. Forgetting faith, forgetting friendship, and joy of love, she climbed the bitter stairs to her top floor, stepping over angry tears and painfully aware in some hidden corner of how scared she was that she had indeed willed him ruination and even death. She had done it to herself. Maybe she had hidden her own devil from herself? She had decided to live and yet there was no joy in her when she thought of him today, no warmth, no soft turning of the heart toward their time together, but a closed spirit slammed shut with refusal to remember, not how, but why she had opened to him. In all her refusal to die for him, there was still something behind that door.

The attic was safe. Sanction of antique junk that had seen enough to absorb any perversion, any hurt and anything you were afraid to admit somewhere else. And no one would know you were home.

She gazed into the street below, with its normality which was often comforting, and which cooperated with her today by looking one-dimensional, and stagelike. Not really there, but *there*, to fill up your empty spaces just enough to push you away from hysteria.

When would she ever leave it—him—herself, behind? Did these ancient loves just go on and on through all of life or did you get to a point, finally, when it didn't matter anymore— what you had in your head didn't matter? The anger didn't matter, the hurt, the confusion, the memories—none of it would matter? Nothing would remind you of anything, anyone else, nothing would nag at your backbone and return to burn its nasty little fire again. Nothing to remind you you were in some ways still struggling with your own poison. Maybe if she could just get old enough, that would happen. Maybe. Anyone passing by who just happened to look up, might have seen a brown face, handsome in its contours, worrying its outline. The glass pane obscured the hair and neck and you could just barely make out the soft eyes. Those who believed in spirits would have been convinced that "Miss Florice had 'haints' " and an unkillable rumor would have bellowed and grown in the small town way, forever. But it was about seven on a southern September and most folks were cleaning up after supper. Save one small person, who was, not untypically, late for her meal. The tears were lost to the dust and glare as she wanted them to be, and the brow leaned against the glass in part despair and part relief at being alone with its old grief. Vaguely aware of Ronnie swinging down the street, she moved aside and sat down on the old trunk she had brought from New Orleans so long ago, so as not to be seen in the twilight. Light was now faint, but she didn't care to be recognized. Suddenly, a rock hit the window with enough force to crack it and glass crashed brilliantly, into the dim attic and onto the floor. Florice almost cried out, but she had half expected something, having seen the twelve-year-old's slingshot. She composed her face quickly, leaned through the place where the pane had been, and glared a spanking at her godchild. Ronnie stood for a moment as if transfixed. She closed her mouth and then did her best to beat the latest high school track record toward home. "Well, she sure broke up those miseries," Florice said to herself, forced to laugh heartily. ". . . 'through a glass darkly, but then face to face . . .' Ha! Saint Paul should have known Ronnie . . . ha!"

1950

Trudy had continued to spend the night and eat at Harriet's table at least once a week for all of her young years. Ronnie forgot to be suspicious and just accepted the lies as a part of Trudy. She even came to share in Trudy's fantasy about "not liking telephones" when they came and took out the phone at Trudy's house; and when Trudy's father died, Ronnie was really sorry she had ever been impatient and wished Trudy would just shut up. They were twelve, and there were lots of scary things ahead and they needed each other's company. It was good to have somebody around who knew you like a sister.

On the way home from school, Ronnie said quietly, "Miss Florice carries the light." Trudy didn't answer. She had a kind of respect for Ronnie. The one who got A's in school; the one who explained things to her. "Did you hear me, Trudy?"

"Yeah, so what's that supposed to mean? You always sayin' somethin' weird."

"Well, she does. I saw it, but I haven't told *nobody*. Folks might think I'm crazy. There's a lot of other things I've seen, too, but I'm not sure anybody else's seen them so I leave it alone. Anyway, she carries it in a circle hangin' on her arm, just like you'd hang a rope for climbin' with."

"Girl, you crazy." Trudy giggled and pushed at Ronnie's arm.

"Don't you tell *nobody*, Trudy. Swear! Swear on your heart and hope to die!!"

"Listen, I ain't swearin' cause Rev Brooks, he say it's a sin. And I ain't hopin' to die, so you kin forget that!"

"Well, you tell anybody, I'm gonna put yo' eyes out at night!" Ronnie always thought of things more horrible to do than Trudy could think of, so that it was a real challenge for Trudy to come up with a counter threat.

"I'm gonna put live worms in yo' bologna sandwich!"

"Yeak!" Ronnie screamed and doubled over in agony. She was laughing wildly. "And I," she said triumphantly, "will tell Charles Gaitha, the cutest boy in school, that your period started last week for first time!"

Trudy was beaten and she knew it. So all she said between gasping for air between giggles, was "Tell me, tell me, girl, about what you don't want me to tell." Since Ronnie had always been an adventure for Trudy, almost anything she said was gospel.

"Well, you know down by the colored funeral home on Pine Avenue?"

"What other funeral home I'm gonna know about, dummy? I ain't turned white overnight, and anyhow I ain't goin' near no funeral home, *no* kinda funeral home. Go on with the story, chile."

"Well, anyhow, I go down there to find stuff sometimes. I can find an old tin can or somethin' to use to practice with my slingshot. Well, you know Miss Florice live down there near the school, and the funeral home's not far. And I was walking home with my slingshot and pickin' up stones and practicin' and I saw these things in Miss Florice's attic window, looked like birds, only they wasn't birds, girl!"

"What'chu see then?" Trudy could hardly stand it.

"Girl, they was bats! And it was 'bout suppertime and you know how bats come out at night. So, I took aim!"

"Oooh girl, I wouldn't mess with Miss Florice. That lady's strange and she mean. What chu do, girl?"

"I didn't mean to break no windows, not really, I mean. Took off runnin', down past Miss Susie Mae's, past the grocery store where that man worked who did that thing to Maye, and as far as I was not afraid to go. Anyhow, behind that windowpane was what scared me. That was when I saw the light."

Trudy stopped chewing her gum for a few minutes. She

was deep in thought. They had almost reached her aunt's house. Trudy and her mother had "moved out to redecorate" their house and somehow had never moved back in. "Miss Florice was standin' in the window, she was just standin' there and this light spread all over her like a dream. I mean, girl, I was scared."

"Aw shit, you ain't seen nothin' but a light; she musta turned on a light." Trudy's eyes were saying something else, but she was playing it cool. "But Trudy," Ronnie whispered now, "there's no electricity up there in her attic. I been up there."

"You think she's a witch?" Trudy's eyes were really stretched wide now.

" '*Course* not. She Mama Florice, my godmother."

"I ain't tellin nobody. I swear I ain't. You right. They say we crazy for sho!" Trudy was on her front stoop. "See ya, girl, see ya tomorrow."

Ronnie wasn't sure she had done the right thing by telling Trudy, and that night she asked God to help Trudy keep her mouth shut. It sure helped to tell somebody, but she knew what it was—a rainbow, just like after the rain—like a beautiful sleeve it was, only there wasn't an old dress from the trunks and things up there. Ronnie was up under her sheet, trying to figure this out. She couldn't wait to see Miss Florice tomorrow. Maybe it would still be there! She shivered with anticipation and a little fear. Mama had called her to breakfast three times the next morning before she bounced up, determined never to aim at any windows, bats or not, and having decided she might really have to be good, like Sunday school good, because that might be a sign of something, that thing with Miss Florice. Anyhow, she'd look today, to see if it was still there. She clattered down the hall to fish and grits. Somehow, she had to find a way to see Miss Florice in the dark again.

The eggs are small, usually hard-shelled units that can be placed by the female where they will have the best chance of survival.

1950

He had been the child she never gave Mac, the child she never gave Robert Brown, the man she had most wanted to have children by. He had been hers for a change, not a lover who belonged to the church, not a friend who belonged to a man as wife, not the child of another woman, but finally hers. She put herself into taking care of one who had come to her, she felt, as a gift. The word had come at church, that there was a child who needed a home. A child whose mother was unknown, but who had been shifted from woman to woman all of his few years. The agency people were looking for still another home. The church was contacted and Florice wanted the child more than anyone suspected. She took the bus to the office downtown, and said yes, she would take him. The white woman behind the desk had said what she had to say with her most perfunctory mouth. ''Now his mother was a common woman, you realize, and she has just disappeared just disappeared, I believe there was some talk about a rape but I'm sure you people would know more about that than I do he's about six and a half years old and he shouldn't give you any trouble you'll get your monthly allowance on time and as long as you don't give us any trouble we won't give you any there's no record of his relatives there didn't seem to be anybody who would be responsible for him you know what I mean now he's a puny little thing so you shouldn't have to spend much for food we will be around often to check on him just sit right here I'll get the boy . . .''
He became hers, at least to her. A child with few expectations and less experience with real love, he began to grow beautiful under her, not knowing why he was so favored, but

147

taking this love in, a thirst-starved seedling. He lost his nervousness, but not his quietness. His smile became real. The year was full of yearnings tried out and fulfilled. It was all right to want a second helping; it was all right to want being tucked in and to want to tuck in. It was permission to cook for someone and to sing someone to sleep, and permission to ask for a song.

Her knowledge that he had Alice's eyes was something she never shared with anyone, and only in trembling with herself. Maye had been lost to them as if taken by death, and there were no accurate records that proved the child was Alice's grandson. More frightened of knowing than of not knowing, Florice ministered to her friend across the abyss of death, and tried to ignore the possibility that they would take him away which was always there. She had no claim to him except her signature.

The answer to her fear came in a letter one morning, one of the few times she didn't know ahead of trouble that trouble was on its way. The letter with heading "Bureau of Children's Services" on a long white sheet. She almost didn't have to read it. "Regret to inform you . . . no male image or presence . . . adoption out of the question . . . removed to a more normal situation . . ." the long page shook. She dialed the agency number with her free hand.

"But Florice, you so *good* with him." Harriet's eyes were full of sympathetic tears. "It's just no justice in this world, no justice. God knows, he's your child." She put out her hand and covered the hand of her friend, wishing there were words, not knowing how to say what she felt. Florice was toiling upward on a stony mountain, pitching boulders at unseen enemies and needing to get to the top; she said nothing.

"Well, can't we *do* something," cried Harriet. "Can't we *do some*thing? You ain't no common woman. Just because you ain't married. Just because you don't have a man next to you in bed at night, they gonna take that boy's only home? And God know's that's how it usually is. I don't mean no harm, but, men, they just home long enough to bring a empty stomach. Ain't no father ever *raised* no chile I know about.''

Her sense of indignation was desperately helpless. A little whimper escaped from her clenched lips and she watched the best friend she had die a little more. Florice shook her head slowly. "Don't fret yourself, Harriet. I'll be goin' now." Harriet raised one hand in a futile protest, but it was pointless to say any more.

He had stayed thin. She would remember the leg, arm, hand, the back, the neck a delicate brown, an old child who spoke little but always to the point, which was maybe why she loved him so much. His features were African. He was not considered a "pretty child" by the narrow standards, and he had what her mother had said was ordinary hair which meant it was not straight or even remotely curly but nappy African. The eyes were deeply brown and serene. Perhaps somewhere there was the shadow knowledge that he was the child of rape and tragedy. Florice hoped not, she hoped he would never know, but someone would no doubt tell him with great sympathy and equal malice and he would be forced to face their guilt and his own and to come some way to live with the shame of being unwanted by either mother or father. In the time she had, Florice had wanted to give enough warmth to cover over the iceberg she knew he carried around. She had waited with dread for the question he would eventually ask someone. Luckily for her it would be asked of someone else somewhere down the road. Rebecca Florice became his temporary calm, his place of refuge, and yet he always knew it would end and the cold would come back. Before her there had been many "not mamas" and many hours of solitary waiting and strange men who patted him, usually on the head and once in a place he wouldn't ever want to talk about. His "not mamas" he called them—there had been four or five, he could never remember which. One smelled always of a golden liquid she kept under the sink and she would drink it from a glass on the kitchen table while he ate his lunch. He didn't remember how he had cried once all night to be changed, and had finally fallen asleep in exhaustion and in filthy pants but he had done it.

Then there was not mama Nancy who always said "remember I'm not your mama" and after he had never forgot he was different, and called them all his not mamas. Nancy was large and warm and gruff, and he was never hungry with her, but she didn't want-no-kid-on-a-full-time-basis and when he had cried three weeks to stay with her it was the last time he ever cried. When he decided not mamas would always go away soon, he felt better; he never shed tears again. When Florice had had to tell him they were taking him, he said, "People always go away, not-mama, you no different" and his eyes were far far away from her.

They had said she wasn't married, with no man in the house the boy wouldn't have a "normal situation." They had said "suitable for a well-rounded adjustment to complete his socialization." The words were carved in a corner of her mind permanently.

We see beauty not so much when she languishes in peace, as when she burns in fierce diamond brilliance, forever, hard as steel. And the fire pains, so that we may know the glory of it. The moon shone as if lit from inside and not from the sister light it borrowed. It seemed to her eyes the message of an eternity waiting. Silver covered the steps, the woodpile, slithered around tree trunks and under the curled edges of the leaves. Where was she now, Alice Wine? Who had loved the moon's light so dearly and seemed to Florice to be the answer when she the soother wanted healing herself? Oh, Alice, help, she thought. Where are you? Are you somewhere in a chair turned toward the evening star, sitting on the wind? Catch my echo, Alice. Come down with this moonlight and bring me some answers, some peace. Why had God taken her only friend? For friend she had been, clean, full, deep, and of another time and place. Florice shook against the southern wind and gripped her own arms. I can't do this alone. Teach me, Lord, teach me. She bit the words through her full lips and stared at the tears in the cup of her hand for a long time. The moon came in through her bedroom window and glimmered on the moisture. Catch my echo, Alice, she prayed, catch it.

Florice had dressed him tenderly for the occasion. Bending over to tie his shoelaces, she felt sick, and ran for the bathroom, so that the boy looked puzzled and wondered what terrible thing was about to happen now. Would this nice mama he had depended upon for a year really let him leave her? He had come to protect himself against feeling, and only the fear was left.

But they did come and they did take him away, and though she said she would find out where he was and visit him, by the time the car door was shut between them, he had returned to his silent place. He would forget her, he would forget her he would he would.

Harriet had stayed away for the leave-taking. She knew her friend. Around nine-thirty she decided it was time to pay a visit. Enough time had gone by for Florice to have done whatever she needed to do to be Florice for one more day. Soon she was walking up the front walk with Ronnie at her side. They rang the bell and waited. October leaves scratched at their legs in the wind. Ronnie had her own grief, having enjoyed the silent little boy, teaching him, reading to him and practicing motherhood.

After what seemed a long time, Florice opened the door. Harriet saw what no one else would ever see. The clothes were in place. The hair was just as neat as usual. Only the eyes were cracked like a thin surface of ice when the temperature is just freezing.

"Good mornin'. How're y'all this morning?" They proceeded as if nothing unusual had happened. Through toast and coffee, through eggs and homemade preserves.

Ronnie wandered into the living room. She was desolate and afraid to show it, knowing that her tears would completely crack that ice covering Miss Florice's eyes. Lost in her young sense of loss, she wandered in the familiar room, touching objects known to her since birth. A picture of someone in New Orleans, a porcelain-headed doll. She picked at a pillow, beautiful with needlepoint, a black butterfly, done on a blue background. All at once she realized she had never seen it before. On impulse she carried it into the kitchen. "Miss Florice, did you make this?" Florice said yes, with a nod. "Well, it sure is pretty," said Ronnie. "Could you teach me? I mean, how to do this? Could you?"

When had she been able to deny this child anything? With

half a mind, Florice said she'd be glad to teach her needle-point, and Ronnie, realizing she'd hit on something that might make her godmother smile again, said, "OK, I'll come over every Saturday after my chores, OK, Mama?" and without waiting for permission she went on rambling about how she would like to make a butterfly and how she would like to start it today and could they go down to Market Street and get the things they needed now? Florice cupped Ronnie's chin and said, "Girl, you more like me than you have any business bein'."

Somewhere the temperature rose just a little, and the October ice thawed. They proceeded.

Frogs, lizards, bats and other small animals eat butter-flies directly as do spiders and predatory insects such as praying mantids, ground beetles, ants, wasps, and hor-nets. Many are killed by the so-called parasitic wasps and flies, of which there are thousands of species.

1954

The line between freedom and slavery is thinner than eggshell cracks, an invisible snag, as obscure, as elusive as spiders' web; but strong, that strong that teaches human need. Within an ace we cannot see it. Knowing it's there gives us cause for great agony and yet we spend our whole lives trying to step over that line, blindly following instinct, not knowing why or how or whether there is, in fact, any difference on the other side once we find the crack in time. She knew she would go tomorrow. To step across this line is terrifyingly simple, always frightening, always complicated; and always angels sing. It remained only for her to say goodbye.

She had had a hard time keeping her pain from them. Ronnie and Harriet were her family now and they knew every line of her face, every slight droop of her shoulders. If she sighed too many sighs they would look at her hard, waiting for an explanation. The pains in her chest had turned from subtle to sharp. The doctor had said two weeks, a month. She had told no one. There was business in Pittsburgh to see about, but mostly there was Robert. She was going to see him one more time if her body held out, if God allowed it. Somehow, she had to say the goodbye she had denied him the day he had left her standing in the kitchen, bitter and wounded.

Greensboro bus station was crowded with college students going home from spring vacation. Their chatter ranged from what they would eat at home to the Supreme Court decision on segregation. She heard and smiled, knowing it wouldn't make any difference to her and maybe not to anyone else. Her steps were deliberate but not heavy. She had seen the

153

spider's web and she knew where she had to step. In line behind a young boy going to Richmond whose youth was a trifle too shiny, she thought, "I have lived, I have lived a long, long time."

"Lady?"

"Two tickets, please. Greensboro to Pittsburgh, Pennsylvania. And Pittsburgh to North Carolina. Jacksonville, North Carolina."

She had a change of clothes and the yellow dress she had worn to the circus. With the daisies on it. She had fit these into a small overnight case. Harriet had been adamant about a coat. "It will be cold up there; now you know I'm right, Florice. You'll come back here with a cold, sure!" She had known more than she wanted to know, and was busy ignoring what she knew. "Lord knows why you goin' way up there at your age by yourself. You ought to let me send Ronnie with you. Wait till school is out and take her. She'd be just excited to go! But I do know you a stubborn woman, Rebecca Florice. Always have been, always will be, I reckon. If you'd have told Ronald you had property to see to, I coulda asked him to go, 'fore he got started on this new shift. Why all the time I didn't know you had property up north!" And so they parted. One chattering to keep up her courage and quiet the fears, and one simply smiling and patting the other on the shoulder.

"Take care, girl, now. You look after that bronchitis you have while I'm gone, you hear?"

"Hurry home, Florice, and you be careful. Them folks wild up north."

Ronnie had been feeling something for a long time. She knew. This trip was important. The last day and she knew how to carry grief the way only the young do. In the taxi next to the woman who had *been*, always, to her, always being, always having been and always going to be, her eyes were wide with fear and knowledge. Her mouth was dry. There were no questions and no explanations. There was nothing to say to one who had taught her all she knew about pain and sunlight. She blinked desperately. They sat in silence and the cab driver rattled on about how warm it was for this time of year and he sure wished he was taking a trip because this cab was drivin' him and he had been a cab driver too long.

The front door looked overpowering like the entrance to a cave or the last stop on your way to some unknown place for prisoners. Ronnie hesitated, dreading the step out of the cab, for this was truly the end. Florice had taken out of her purse a small black finger-worn change holder that was too familiar to Ronnie. Something about the black leather, the click a sit opened the click a sit closed, something made her almost drop her control. Ronnie was holding on to that purse with everything she had. She heard a voice say, "Wait here for her, please, sir. She'll be right back." Ronnie saw five dollars in her hand. Way too much for the ride home. The voice said, "Come on. Let's go in." Ronnie saw the purse disappear into a larger purse, and finally she came back to herself, and took Miss Florice's arm. The older and the younger, holding on to each other, walked slowly into the bus station. They were both aware that the greatest lies are those we agree not to tell each other.

When she climbed back into the backseat of the taxi, Ronnie realized that Florice had not really said goodbye. She had said "be good," and "take care of yourself." She had kissed her on both cheeks, and climbed the steps onto the bus, and waved, but she had never said "goodbye." Ronnie clung to that like a drowning person gripping a buoy. She prayed, she hoped she was right. Maybe her godmother would be back after all. Then she had an inspiration. The rainbow must be made of hope! That was it, hope! When she came back Ronnie would have the answer. She settled back in the seat, doing a very good job ignoring her own truth. She put her hands in her pockets. Some kind of paper was there. She pulled it out. It was the song about the rainbow. The whole conversation at the park came flooding back, and Ronnie knew she had the right answer, the answer was hope, but it was hope for her, for *her* future, and Mama Florice was truly "goin' home." As the cab pulled up at her house, she wondered how much her mama knew about this. She guessed she'd keep it to herself. That's what Mama Florice would do.

She shook a little as she paid the cab driver, and walked around to the back door so she could sit on the steps by herself until Mama came home.

* * *

Florice had taken her to the park the day before she left. They had walked through the woods. The spring mud smelled good, like the clean green things soon to come. A few early crocuses showed their heads. Ronnie was almost a young lady now, her natural tomboyishness was beginning to be lost. Florice sighed, wishing young things could stay young, knowing why they couldn't. Ronnie was very quiet, waiting. A little frightened, aware there was going to be some kind of sadness to come.

"So how's my honey today?" Florice looked at her quickly, and looked away as they walked through the park. "Got some young man on your mind?" She knew Ronnie was feeling the future and she knew how uncomfortable that could be. "Nothing to say, is that what it is? Let's see, let's play our old game of questions. You ask me whatever you want to ask me that you've always wanted to ask, and I'll try to answer it. And then I get to ask you."

Ronnie was counting the number of squirrels and birds she had seen so far. It was better than thinking so much and being so scared. Three squirrels and three birds. And what did she most want to know? Without thinking, it slipped out, just rolled off her tongue without her permission. "Why are you goin' away, really?" she said, still looking for squirrels and birds. "Four," she added quickly.

"Four what?"

"Four birds, I'm counting birds."

"Oh. Well, you asked and I promised to answer. Got to go see an old friend of mine who's sick. Don't know if he'll make it through this time. Also, my sister had property up there. Got to go take care of some business. Now I got a question for you. What you think a rainbow is made of?"

Ronnie stopped chewing on some gum she had in her mouth, and threw it away.

"Easy answer! Light and water. You could have made it harder you know."

"Wrong," said Florice smiling.

"Wrong?" Ronnie shook her head. "No, I know that's right."

"Well, you just think about it. You'll figure it out. You always did. You'll get this one. You tell me when you do." Ronnie looked amused and puzzled.

"OK, next question. Why would God give us rainbows?"

"That's not hard at all. To make us happy," she said. "You know, like with colors and flowers. You know, Mama Florice, sometimes I talk to God in my dreams and He tells me things. Jesus too. Isn't that funny?" She didn't stop for an answer. It was as if she wanted to be sure she said all these things today, and they just came tumbling out in a nervous rush. "When I was about twelve, I saw that rainbow on your arm right there on your shoulder, and you didn't know it but I saw it when you were in the attic that day I shot out the window. And I was afraid to tell anybody. I was even afraid to tell you, and so I only told Trudy and she never told anybody. Sometimes I can see it and sometimes I can't though. Why is that?"

Florice wasn't really surprised at the rush of questions. She knew it was time. "Because your windows to God aren't always open all the way."

Ronnie stopped on the path for a minute. Then she started walking again slowly. Something rustled in the leaves nearby. Another bird.

"Will they ever be?"

"One day they probably will be," said her godmother. "It's something you can't control. It's up to God. You may be able to heal folks or you may just be able to see the future. You'll know when you know. It's nothing to play with, Ronnie. You got to ask God for help every day and He will show you the way. And don't forget, if you say yes to God, you got to give it all." Florice knew that Ronnie wouldn't fully understand all of this now, but that someday in the future the words would come back to her when she most needed them.

Ronnie's eyes were wide open and her spine kind of tingled. Would she really be able to make people well someday? The future. The future. Was that what she was seeing when she had these strange feelings about Mama Florice? She kept feeling something about sickness and hospitals. She desperately wanted to ask another question about the trip up north to Pittsburgh, but she didn't dare at the same time. Something told her she wouldn't want to know the answer. All this stuff was scary and exciting all mixed up together. It was very quiet in the woods. The snakes were still hibernating, and the tall pines gave off their biting sweetness. Ronnie could feel her fear, a little spring wound up in her stomach. She knew that the real reason for this walk in the park had not been mentioned and she bit her lips to keep from crying. They turned back toward the main area of the park.

Miss Florice finally broke the silence. "One thing is certain, honey, you got these gifts for a reason, 'cause God don't waste His gifts on anybody. You got to trust the Lord to tell you what to do and say. Everything you do, you got to trust. You know, Ronnie, God gave me a great opportunity to serve, but I don't think I ever saw it all the way through." She sighed. "I guess I did the best I could; it was never easy for me, but maybe it'll be easier for you. It's a different world now. Things are changin' fast."

They had reached the edge of the woods. Florice took both of Ronnie's hands in hers. "I hope you'll find a man who'll make you happy, so you won't have to be so different, and so alone all your life. It's hard enough just bein' different."

Ronnie hugged her godmother. "I'll be fine, Mama Florice. I'll be just fine."

Her young eyes were glistening in the spring wind which had suddenly broken the calm. There was a rain whipping itself up. How young she is, thought Florice, how young for such a glorious burden. She prayed silently for her safety, for her sanity. Out loud, she said, "Before we go, I got one more thing to say to you," and she rustled in her coat pocket for a piece of paper. "These are the words to an old song I used to hear down in New Orleans, way before you were ever thought of. The men on the road gangs used to sing to keep their minds from going bad. I couldn't remember it all, but I've been wanting to give you at least what I remember, and this seems like a good time to give it to you; you're almost sixteen now, almost a woman."

Ronnie read the words to herself.

> Evahwhuh I, whuh I look dis mawnin
> Looks lak rain, looks lak rain.
>
> I gotta rainbow, tied all roun mah shoulder
> Ain gonna rain, ain gonna rain.
>
> I'm gonna break right, break right pas dat shooter
> I'm goin home, Lawd, I'm goin home.
>
> I gotta rainbow, tied all roun mah shoulder
> Ain gonna rain, ain gonna rain.

The trees were shaking now, and they could really smell the rain. Ronnie looked up at her special godmother. She almost said, Are you going up there for an operation? Are you sick, Mama Florice? But she was too afraid of the answer. It just couldn't be. It just couldn't be that she wouldn't see her after tomorrow. She pushed this as far back in her mind as she could but there was just nowhere for it to hide. The fifth bird broke free of the trees.

"Mama Florice, you'll have another time to talk to me. It's going to rain. Let's hurry!" The rain had caught them. As they reached her father's car, Ronnie was very glad that the rain had completely soaked her face.

* * *

Pittsburgh was dry. Gray. Fut, fut, she thought. Fut fut fut fut. That was the sound it made for her. Gray sky, gray trees, gray pavement, black and gray and tan cars, and black and gray and tan people. The South, now that is where you should live for color, she thought. The suitcase, fut fut fut against her leg. All it contained was a yellow daisy dress and a small flowerpot, some seeds, a toothbrush, comb, and bar of soap. Everything went fut fut. Within it and without it. That included her oxfords and her spring coat which flapped around her knees in the city wind.

The Stevedore, it said in front. Well, in the Negro section of town you couldn't be too choosy. Still, there might be a YWCA for colored girls. She walked on. Decided to phone. The booth was empty in the early morning. Folks goin' to work ain't got time to make no calls. Always did hate diggin' for pennies in a handbag. She thought of Ronnie's face in a flash of pain, opened the black change purse, and slipped a coin into the phone. It rattled to its destination and the operator answered with a northern crispness she found abrupt. The YWCA did have rooms for colored. On 26th and East Northwood. Take the bus. Three dollars a night. Thank you.

There'd be a prayer meetin' tonight, and Wednesday, early evenin' choir practice. Tomorrow morning would do fine. The Rev. Robert Brown, 12th Street, A.M.E. Zion Church. Won't need the phone number. 12th Street A.M.E. Zion, that's enough. It was Wednesday afternoon. The room was small and warm, and that was good. Nothin' I hate worse'n bein' cold. She thought of Bear Island. Well, that's that anyhow. I already decided that. Still, Harriet had been right. It was good to have a coat. She sat down at the little desk and looked for paper and a pencil. There was no pencil in the drawer.

She had to call that lawyer about the house she wanted to leave to Ronnie. There was no phone in the room. She'd use the one in the lobby, and then go to bed. She had to be careful so she wouldn't give out before seeing Robert.

Sleep would finally come that night but not easily. Anyway, she thought, there'd be no end of it soon enough. Maybe not, though, maybe not. What was it like, really? She wondered. She was a little nervous, wishing for some chamomile tea to sooth her nerves. Darkness, no feeling, or all light and welcoming angels? Probably not either one, she thought. Like dreaming, maybe like dreaming. Maybe we see those who have gone ahead. She thought of her mother for the first time in a long time. Her mother. New Orleans. Darkness.

* * *

Crazed—three steps up and you could see, just barely, out the window; three steps down and it was impossible to reach the trash can. There were two pinned butterflies on the wall, still fluttering, alive. No water in the mop bucket. Her mother carefully mopped the floor. Slightly out of place, a crooked picture, a rug with wavy edges that threatened to trip you. The bird was standing on the dining room table, on one foot, and she could see an injured wing. He was a sea bird, maybe a sandpiper. She tried catching; frightened, it took off, crashing into the first wall it came to. Falling to the floor, taking off, falling to the floor in a heap. She felt the wing pain crack in her shoulder. God, please let me catch you, she moaned to herself. Her mother said, coldly, "In New Orleans, we used to have things fixed so that nothing could get in. You should have put that chicken wire across the chimney." She went on mopping very carefully with her dry mop. The bird had found a window, mistaken the coolness for the outside, and was straining and fluttering its wings, over and over again, against the pain. "No . . . no," she said to her dream. Running to the door, holding it open, she said, "*Now*, it's open I've got it open for you; this way." It was dark midnight. "Go on. Go on out there and fly in the night." The bird smelled the air and slipped over it into the night, flying on one good wing.

* * *

She had felt a little pain in the night, but not as much as last week. Didn't matter. After all these years, she knew when God was playing and when He was serious.

Puttin' on her shoes was strange. Could be the last time I put shoes on, she thought. That made her a little sad, but she was too anxious to leave Pittsburgh to think much about it. The bus was scheduled to pull out at 9:00. It was 7:00 and she had to find that church. Downstairs, young girls were slowly getting ready for work. She had worn the same dress she had on yesterday but it was clean she thought. She had rinsed it out in the shared bathroom last night.

"Well now, mornin, ma'am. Ain't you up early? Yes ma'am. Now les see, 12th Street, Mt. Zion."

"Mt. Zion A.M.E." Florice said clearly. She had to make that bus.

"That's not too far from here." The janitor was in starched overalls and was concentrating more on his own curiosity than on the directions he was giving. "You can't miss it," he said at the top of his voice. "You can't miss it." The large wooden door closed. Florice thought, "Mister, you'd be surprised what I can miss." Including the bus, she said to herself, with a turned down smile.

The church was rather small and worn and stood on a busy street corner that was in a poor section of the city. He had come to this to avoid a life with her. She felt sorry for him, and shame at her long years of anger. 7:25. She tried the church door. It was open. The janitor was just coming in to work. Florice adjusted her suitcase.

"Excuse me, would the Rev Brown be in?"

"Not today, ma'am. He's still in the hospital. You a stranger here?"

"Is he very sick?" She looked down at her suitcase and sighed. She was very tired.

"Well, ma'am, I don't know for sure, but they tell me he may not make it this time. It's his heart. We sho hope he do. He's a good man, Rev Brown."

"What hospital, please?"

"Ma'am?"

"What hospital is he in?"

"St. Luke's, ma'am."

"Thank you. Could you tell me how far it is?"

"I'll call you a cab, ma'am. Too far for you to walk." 7:40. If she went to the hospital, she'd miss the bus. "Yes, thank you. Thank you. That would be good." She was feeling a little pain now, and glad for the rescue. There was, after all, no need for panic. She reckoned God could wait a little longer.

He was on the second floor. Room 212. She asked for a visitor's pass and told them she was his sister from North Carolina and would only be in town for the day. There was a ''no visitors'' sign on the door and a crucifix above that. She stood outside for a few minutes, rubbing the handle slowly to get herself together to see the man she had so deeply loved and to prepare herself that he might be wasted, thin, and not able to recognize her. Finally she pushed it open. He was asleep. The I.V. tube hung limply from his arm. He looked very much as he had in 1940, only, gray and very thin. She caught her breath and stopped her hand. He was very ill. She found a chair and brought it near the bed. It was the kind of chair hospitals use to make an attempt at comfort, covered with a cold crackling vinyl. She sat down, and put her suitcase near her. It was 8:15 A.M. He stirred slightly. His skin was very black on the white sheets and his cheekbones stood out in clear relief. She leaned over to listen. He was only dreaming. After a few minutes of prayer, Florice opened her suitcase and took out the flowerpot and the daisy dress. She unwrapped the rag from around the pot, and shook the loose dirt back in it. Then she reached into her suitcase and from the side pocket, brought out a small envelope which contained basil seeds, and pushed them down in the dirt. A glass of water for the seeds would do. She wrapped the sleeves of her old daisy dress around the pot and left it trailing on the floor next to the bed. Now, a pencil, or pen. She looked in the suitcase, and finally she gave up and opened the top drawer of the nightstand.

She would have seen her own name anywhere, but there was no missing it in Robert's handwriting. Addressed to her. In North Carolina. Stamped. Never mailed. Why would he have brought it to the hospital, except he thought of mailing it, or maybe he thought it would be found after his death? Her hand trembled a little. The paper was slightly soiled. She opened it with eagerness and fear. It was dated August 3, 1942. My darling Rebecca, she read,

I can't stand the pain without you. How did this happen? I knew you would think it hadn't meant anything to me. I was trapped. I couldn't find a way out. Please hear me. Please finish this letter. I can't bear being without you anymore. If you say the word, I will leave her and send for you. I left you because I was afraid that I could not hold out, that I would lose Jessie, you, and the church. That I would lose myself. My life is a prison. I feel tight, constricted. I cannot love Jessie. We must find a way together. Now I know that if we aren't together, I will not have anything. I will lose it all anyhow. Please don't hate me. Come to me. You were right. Oh God, you were right that day in your kitchen. I didn't have the courage to be who I was. We were supposed to be together. If you cannot come, please forgive me. I cannot go on, knowing you believe that I scorned you and your love. God bless you always.

Forever, your Robert

Twelve years; they could have had twelve years together. Oh Lord, why hadn't he sent it? She wanted to shake him awake, even now, to make his pain go away at last. Jessie had finally left and still he hadn't sent it. She must have known she wasn't loved. She had to have known. And why hadn't he sent it then? She had to hold on just a little longer. Too much to feel now. Now that it was truly too late. But she could still forgive and she could give whatever was hers to give, and if God had any mercy at all, Robert would know before he died that she had finally understood his fear. That she understood why he didn't trade that pretty prison of respectability for her, and now she knew why she hadn't forgiven him. It was because they both wanted the same thing. A prison. A protected nest, a place where their differences could hide, and with him she would have been protected from herself. And he wouldn't do it; he wouldn't leave his own sanctuary. My God, she thought, that fear is such a great one. And what did I think a man and children would do for me? Keep me from being what I was bound to be anyway? I blamed him for failing me because I couldn't forgive myself for failing

God. The tears were streaming down her face. I must help him, she thought. At least I can do that now. She collected herself, wiped her face, and looked around to see where the nurses were. They had finished their morning rounds at 8:15. No one was in sight except a lone nun who walked the halls silently. Florice began to concentrate all her energy on Robert, his face, his heart. She leaned over and placed her hands on his chest. She wanted to be free of the burden that had made it so heavy for so long—this Light she carried. And her heart was satisfied at last, at last, as she felt the energy leave her and permeate his body. The rainbow was as bright as it had ever been in this one final blaze of healing. It settled some, and glowed around her body like a bright mist on a winter morning.

She felt so drained. Tired. She began to gather her coat and suitcase realizing she had never found a pen to write him a note. It didn't matter now, he would know.

As she stood over him saying goodbye, he opened his eyes slowly. At first there was no conversation. Only a slow recognition that she was there. And in that peace, she felt his hand on her arm. "You did it, didn't you?" He barely whispered. "I feel stronger."

She only nodded. "Not me. I found the letter and I do forgive you, I do understand."

"But . . ."

"No," she put her hand on his lips. "I expected more of you than I was willing to give, even to God. That's not fair. Now sleep. You need to sleep. I must go," she said. "God has called me." He held her hand tightly. "Take the pot home with you and use the holy basil. It's good for you. You must get well and finish your work. I will see you on the other side." She bent over and kissed him lightly and he closed his eyes again. He did not want to watch her go.

Some species mimic other life forms through the use of color and form to protect themselves. Other moths have no defenses, but protect themselves by imitating those who do.

On her way home. Home to the most beautiful place she had ever seen. The bus stopped in Petersburg, a change for those going to the North Carolina coast. One more leg to this journey and she'd be there. She took an unfinished letter to Ronnie out of her handbag. The layover gave her time to finish it and put it in the bus station mailbox.

To Miss Ronnie Johnstone
72 North Ebner Street
Greensboro, North Carolina
March 23, 1954

My Dear Dear Goddaughter,

I've thought a long time about how to say this to you. Maybe I've thought about it all my life, I don't know. You are my special child, blessed with some of God's most wonderful and dangerous gifts. I think we have talked a lot about some of them. You can see what is going to happen in the future better than I can, and you know what other folks need before they do. We've talked about that too. This means that you will have a glorious and wonderful life, my lovely baby. But it means most that God wants you to do something for Him. You knew when I left you that I would not be coming back home. It is my time. I hope you do not cry too much, for it comes to us all, and I will be with you wherever you are. I thought that what I would leave you as I went home to God was not any of my few things, though you will find a box of treasures if you look under your bed, and the property up north is yours, but mostly I can leave you what I have learned in strugglin' through the fiery furnace. I can leave you some things to carry with you, and to remember.

Remember that God is everywhere. Look for Him when you wake up, all day, and when you go to sleep, but look for Him mostly in your brothers and sisters. Remember that the only difference between you and everybody else is that you have a different job to do than they do. Other folks won't understand that. You may be lonely sometimes. But, you'll never be alone. I want you to remember that God doesn't put nothin' on you you can't bear. Don't be scared, and don't you let nobody turn you around. I think times are going to be hard in the next few years. I think you gonna hafta fight for our people. I can see that coming. But you don't have no reason to fear. The Precious Lord will take your hand, don't you worry.

Remember you got to leave folks to the Lord. You got to soften your heart and forgive folks for what they do to you, 'cause they tryin' hard to live in this world, hard as you, and ain't none of it easy. If you can't forgive, your back will carry heavy burdens you don't need to have. I know.

Remember that love is the only thing that matters in God's world and you got to be about loving folks, so what you got, use it for love. And if you have a love of your own, no matter how short it lasts or how long, you have been blessed, 'cause it don't come easy, it don't come easy at all. One thing I learned when I went to Pittsburgh. Being scared to say yes to love is just like being scared to say yes to God. Don't do what I did, Ronnie. I had a love once who was scared to say yes to me, and we lost each other. And like I told you in the park, when you say yes, you got to give it all, or else it's like breaking a promise. For a long time, I thought I had said yes to God, but I was afraid to trust God with my happiness, so I tried to find it on my own, and I was only fooling myself, 'cause my feet were set on the path by the Lord, and I couldn't help myself and I couldn't turn back. You know, when the tide comes in, it comes in as far as it can. Not halfway today, and maybe all the way tomorrow. But as far as it can every time. You be like the tide, Ronnie, and the Lord will make a way for you, even in the wilderness. Take care of your friends. They are like green pastures in the desert. You will need them.

The Lord will test you every day. I will be there prayin' for you wherever He puts me. Remember when it looks like rain, you got a rainbow tied all roun your shoulder, showing you how to break past trouble and find your way home. Same rainbow that's been hanging on my arm since I was twenty-two years old. It's yours now. From God to me; from me to you. Don't turn it loose now 'cause it'll see you through, it'll light your way in those dark places you got to climb to. You been strong a long time, Ronnie. Jesus laid his hands on you when you come here. You'll be fine. God's rainbow is a promise.

Love always,
Godmama Florice

She turned her back to the sand dunes and walked along the beach for a while. The ferry had left for the night. She was searching for something specific on this beach which was her home.

The great water was a composition of softness. Gray, white, ivory, tan, a bell sound of silver outlined the waves, and they spoke of a gentle and grand music underlaid by the mother heart which never rests. She moved slower and slower, looking patiently until it began to get dark. Had anyone been there, they would have seen the mist around her and decided it was only the evening fog off the ocean. Finally she saw it in the fading light. A half sand dollar. She picked it up, smiling, and pulled out of her coat pocket another half which she had found in 1915, the day Mac ran off. They almost fit. When she put them together, she could see the flower pattern outlined, the five wounds, the delicate star. "The gift of promises broken," she whispered, "the gift of promises kept." She put them both in her right hand, walked toward the ocean, and threw them in.

The wind had become quite cold. There was a small sheltered cove not far ahead. Just before the steel-colored clouds disappeared into blackness, Rebecca Florice settled into a slight depression in the sand. The Light around her shoulders rose to a crystalline incandescence, faded gently, and went out.

There are moths and butterflies in the frozen arctic, in the tropical forests and in the deserts. They range in size from only a few millimeters to over a foot, but they are of great importance in the lives of all plants and animals.

Some are weak flyers, but some are strong enough to fly more than a thousand miles, and are known even to cross oceans.

About the Author

LINDA BEATRICE BROWN, author of *A Love Song to Black Men*, teaches English in Greensboro, North Carolina, at Guilford College. She holds a Ph.D. from Union Graduate School in Cincinnati, Ohio, and has published poetry and lectures as well as fiction, in publications including *The Black Scholar, Religion and Intellectual Life*, and *Ebony Junior*. She frequently gives workshops and lectures on the imagination and the spirit, black studies, and women's studies.